THE LAST THIRTEEN

BOOK EIGHT

JAMES PHELAN

Scholastic Canada Ltd.

Toronto New York London Auckland Sydney
Mexico City New Delhi Hong Kong Buenos Aires

PREVIOUSLY

With the loyal Guardians bravely fighting back against Stella's Agents, Sam and Tobias jump from the bridge in a daring escape. They drive across the US, headed for Eva and Lora, stopping at the home of Tobias' uncle, Duke, in Texas to regroup.

Alex comes up with an ingenious plan and breaks free from the Vancouver compound with his mother. Back at the Academy in London, a chance discovery leads Alex to believe he is one of the last 13. He goes to Washington with a team of Agents to prevent the powerful transceiver concealed within the Monument falling into Stella's hands.

On their way back to the Academy, Eva and Lora are ambushed by Mac's men and have to go on the run across the country. Tracked by a drone plane, they take refuge in the bustle of Las Vegas.

The tranquility of Duke's farm is soon shattered by a surprise attack from Stella. She wants to mine Sam's dreams for all that he knows about the race. While Sam is drugged, Tobias frees them, waking Sam.

In Washington, the Agents mysteriously disappear, forcing Alex to climb the Monument to disable the transceiver alone. Fighting off two Marines, he smashes the top of the Monument and rescues his mother and the Agents from Mac's soldiers.

Using a secret underground passage, Tobias rescues Duke and hijacks Stella's jet, using it to distract their captors while Sam escapes in Duke's vintage Mustang car. He drives to the Grand Canyon, where he meets Cody, the next of the last 13.

Sam and Cody BASE jump into the Canyon, leading them to the hidden temple Cody had discovered and where he says the Gear is to be found. Deep underground, Sam is betrayed by Cody and his Agent parents who have sided with Mac in the race to discover the Dream Gate.

Sam is taken to a government base under Denver Airport. Mac triggers the timer on a nuclear device when Solaris attacks the base, scattering everyone inside. It's too late for Sam to run when Solaris confronts him and changes the countdown, leaving only minutes before the bomb will explode . . .

SAM

05 :55
05:54

Sirens wailed as flashing emergency lights strobed overhead. Sam ran out of the control room into the corridor of the underground complex. There he saw the trail of destruction Solaris had left in his wake. Among the huge chunks of concrete that littered the ground, Sam saw several Marines sprawled on the floor, their bodies at jarring angles. Closest to the door, Mac was slumped over, motionless, his hand still clutching his chest.

Is he out cold? Or is he . . . ?

Sam put his fingers to Mac's neck. No pulse. He struggled to latch onto one emotion as conflicting thoughts ran through his mind.

Mac deserved this end, but still . . .

What about the others?

A severe, robotic voice rang out above the wailing sirens—

"T-minus five minutes until detonation."

"Sam!" a voice called out.

Sam could just make out Cody at the other end of the long corridor, staggering forward with his parents. Despite the smoke haze, their faces were clearly etched with shock and fear. Cody pointed meaningfully toward the outside wall and then waved at Sam, gesturing for him to look at the wall where he stood. He shouted something but Sam couldn't make it out. Sam turned to see a line of doors next to him.

What's behind these doors?

Sam took a small, cautious step forward to read a sign at the nearest door. Two words were printed above an electronic control pad, illuminated by a bright red light:

He looked back to Cody and his parents and saw that the light next to their door was green.

An escape pod must still be in there, ready to go . . .

"Go!" Sam shouted to Cody without thinking, waving wildly. "*Go!*"

Cody hesitated for a moment, then gave a quick nod and hurriedly followed his parents through the open doorway. Sam scanned the corridor. The sirens echoed through the deserted complex. All security personnel had disappeared what seemed like a long time ago, even though only minutes had ticked by.

All the doors close to him showed red lights. If he squinted to see down the still-smoky hallway in the other direction, he could just make out a few tiny green lights in the distance.

Sam went to sprint toward them but suddenly felt a tight grip around his arm.

"No," Solaris said. "*We* stick together."

Sam jumped. He slowly turned back to look at Solaris, fear rising in his throat.

I thought he'd gone, left me for dead.

Sam stood straighter to counter his fear. "To go where?" he said.

Solaris paused, evaluating Sam for a moment. A chunk of rubble near Sam's feet tumbled farther down a pile of blasted concrete. Sparks spat erratically from where live electrical cables dangled from the ceiling.

Without answering, Solaris started to walk down the corridor, dragging Sam behind him.

They navigated around the shattered slabs of concrete

toward the green lights indicating the available escape pods, until they reached a tall mound of collapsed wall, the site of the main explosive impact, which blocked the corridor.

"You first!" Solaris said, pushing Sam ahead of him to climb over the obstruction.

Sam shook off Solaris' grip and started to slowly crawl up and over the pile. Pieces of concrete and debris shifted and slid under him as he tried to make his way over. A live wire sparked and hissed near his face as he made it to the other side.

"Stop!" Solaris commanded, raising his weapon to reinforce the command. Then, as Solaris scaled the rubble with little effort, time seemed to stand still for a few seconds as Sam ran through his options.

There's no way I can outrun him here. I wouldn't make it to the closest pod . . . the live wires . . .

Tobias' science class had the answer—*conductive electricity.*

Sam looked down at his rubber shoes, then back at Solaris, fully clad in his metal body armour, covered in high-tech weapons circuitry.

In one quick motion, Sam took a step toward Solaris, grabbing the wire as he moved to bring it into contact with his enemy's mask—

ZAP!

On connecting with Solaris, a bright blue spark arced in

the air and ran up Sam's hand and arm. He was sent flying backwards with such force that he slammed into the wall several metres away.

Sam scrambled up, trying to move as fast as he could despite being dazed and unsteady on his feet. He looked at Solaris, who had been sent flying even farther in the opposite direction back up the corridor. There was now a sizable distance between them. Sam could see the shimmering black form of Solaris slowly starting to rise . . .

"T-minus two minutes until detonation."

Sam saw another door with a green light. He hit the door release. Inside was a cylindrical-shaped pod, with a bench seat running around the inside. He stepped into the small space, feeling as though he were inside a missile.

The corridor door hissed shut, and Sam heaved the inner pod door closed, spinning the locking wheel as fast as his shaking hands could manage. As the lock slid into place, a tiny screen inside lit up with a command option:

ENTER DESTINATION CODE

Huh? What?

Panicked, knowing Solaris would be at the door in a matter of moments, Sam punched in the first four numbers that came into his head: 1 3 1 3.

CODE ERROR

ENTER DESTINATION CODE

Sam tried again with a set of random numbers.

C'mon! Please work!

DESTINATION CONFIRMED

PRESS TO LAUNCH

Sam exhaled in relief. He leaned over to the launch button and pressed it. Numbers began counting down from ten. As he watched the digits flick by on the screen, he strapped into a four-point harness fastened to the pod wall, his still-shaking hands making him fumble as he did up the clips.

Got no idea where I'm going, but anywhere is better than here.

. . . *5*

4

3

2

1

The noise of the launch was deafening. Sam put his hands over his ears as the escape rockets ignited and the pod shot upward with great speed. There were no windows so Sam had no idea what was happening outside. All he could make out was the immense noise and the feeling of motion as he was pushed down into his seat.

Sam counted the seconds from launch, while trying to remember back to another of Tobias' science classes where they had watched a space rocket launch.

How many kilometres per second was it that they travelled?

He could hear Tobias talking about angles and direction and velocity in his head . . .

Inside the windowless rocket, he kept counting the seconds but then gave up. It was impossible to tell how fast or how far he was travelling.

This is designed to get survivors away from any catastrophe, including a nuclear blast. I'll be a long way away by now . . .

Suddenly, the roaring of the rocket engines petered out, with the pod continuing to glide in a smooth trajectory. Sam tried to relax. He looked around and waited, and listened. There was an odd moment of being suspended mid-air, where he felt weightless.

CLUNK, CLUNK, CLUNK.

Sam heard what he guessed were the rocket booster packs separating from the body of the escape capsule. For the first time the thought of landing entered his mind.

How does this thing touch down? And how will anyone ever find me when it does?

"OK . . . that's OK, I'm sure I'll figure it out when the time comes," Sam said to himself. He felt the speed of the pod starting to increase again. "Except . . . now I'm not flying, I'm just—"

Falling.

Sam froze upright in his seat for a few seconds, listening carefully to the muffled sounds outside the walls. The speed of the dropping capsule continued to pick up until—

BOOMPH!

He felt the jolt of arrested motion as what must have been parachutes were deployed. Immediately, the free-falling descent slowed. Sam relaxed a little back into his seat. He closed his eyes and tried to breathe steadily again.

Nothing to do now but wait . . .

SAM'S NIGHTMARE

"**S**hh, listen," the girl says.

I turn to her.

"Hear that?" she says.

"What?" I say. "I don't hear anything."

A fire flickers in the small fireplace in the middle of the tiny cabin. The flames make me anxious, my heart races, but it is too cold to put the fire out.

"That's what I mean. The wolves are silent."

She's right. A memory of their incessant howls echoes in my mind.

Try to remember, Sam.

We have been asleep, before the wolves started up against the moon, waking us suddenly. Then, just as abruptly, they have stopped.

Silence.

I stand by the locked door, my breath fogging in front of my face. At my feet there's a wet patch seeping in from under the door, where the snow drift outside melts against the wood, warmed by the fire. I look down at the small table by the door. The girl's bag is there, sagging open.

I can see an ID card, sitting on the top, among other papers and spare clothes.

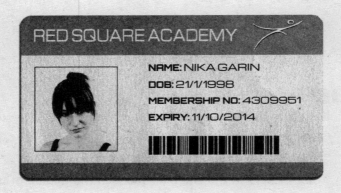

RED SQUARE ACADEMY

NAME: NIKA GARIN
DOB: 21/1/1998
MEMBERSHIP NO: 4309951
EXPIRY: 11/10/2014

The girl walks over to the fireplace and places another log on the fire. The flames jump up higher, making my uneasiness take over my breathing. I try to calm myself.

"But they are still out there. Waiting, planning . . ." she says, her strong accent matching her strong voice.

Planning?

"But we're safe in here?" I say.

"Maybe," she says, now sitting in one of the two battered armchairs in front of the fire. She looks around the room and I follow her gaze. There's a tiny bench at the back of the cabin, serving as a kitchen, separated from the main area by a couple of cupboards. A small fold-away mattress stands pushed against one of the side walls, close to a collection of firewood and fishing equipment.

I press my ear to the front door.

Complete silence still. I preferred hearing the calls of the wolves in the night. Then I could tell roughly how far away they were.

"Maybe they've gone?" I say.

"No."

"Then what would make the pack go quiet like that?"

For a moment, she appears to reflect on the question, perhaps running through the possibilities. The firelight through the steel grill is the only illumination in the room, its orange glow flickering against her striking features.

"It's a big pack," she says, as though thinking it through out loud. "A super pack, they call it, hundreds of them."

"Hundreds?"

She nods. I lean back against the door.

"Something may have disturbed them," she says. "Or it's probably about food—they've been howling to assemble the pack. They're going silent to move in on their prey."

"What do they eat?"

"Meat."

"Any meat?"

"Deer, probably."

"They're going to need a lot of deer. I mean, for hundreds of them? That's a *lot* of deer."

She nods again. "My parents took me through this region once, when I was a little girl," she says. "We would only drive in the daytime and stay in villages for the night."

"Because of the wolves?"

"Because of everything that Mother Nature can deal out around here," she says.

The fire crackles and she watches it, mesmerized.

"One day," she continues, "our vehicle broke down. We were forced to sleep in it for the night. It was very cold, but peaceful. My father stayed up all night, worried. I slept—to me it was a great adventure. I didn't know any better. Then the howling woke me. That sound—it was terrifying. And then it got worse. Then they stopped . . ."

I swallow hard. I turn and press my ear to the door again. The only sound is of the wind being sucked in through the tiny gap at the bottom of the doorframe. I feel tired, and a cold shiver runs through me, up my spine.

She seems all talked out. I want to ask her what happened next, but I don't.

"First light," she says, "we will leave."

I'm too distracted to respond as the silence outside is broken.

The crunching of feet upon snow.

I tense and listen. The girl has heard it too.

"What is it?" she asks.

"Shh!" I say, and listen hard.

More footsteps. Distant, but moving closer. Moving quickly, nearing.

"Someone's coming." I back away from the door until I'm standing next to her and the fire is close behind me.

"Someone?" she says, getting to her feet. "Or some*thing*?"

BANG! BANG! BANG!

The thick wooden door shakes in its rough-hewn wooden frame. The door is old, but solid. The lock is a sturdy slide-across metal bar. There's only one window in the cabin, boarded over, inside and out, to shut out the worst of the harsh weather. A small metal chimney disappears through a round cut-out in the ceiling.

BOOM! BOOM! BOOM!

The pounding against the door is louder now, as if whoever is out there is using some kind of battering ram. The hinges won't hold out for long and neither will the metal bar. They'll get through.

"There has to be another way out of here!" I say.

At the sound of my voice, the pounding stops. Silence. We both stand, unmoving.

"Have they gone?" she whispers.

"No," I reply. "Whoever is out there wants us more than the hungry wolves. They need us for this race. They will be planning too."

There's a huge *WHACK!* against the door.

I frantically glance around the room again, panicked.

Maybe . . .

"Help me," I say to her. Together, we use the fire poker to dig at a joint between two of the wide floorboards, and soon we have the metal bar through. We lean on it to pry up one of the boards. It comes free, leaving a gap to the space

under the floor. The gap is no more than fifteen centi-
metres wide. Not big enough to get through.

"We need to pull up another one!" she says.

"I know." I squat down and put my fingers under the
wooden plank and try to stand, lifting with all the strength
in my body.

It doesn't move—

Another *WHACK!* against the door. A huge crack splits
the middle panel. The sound reverberates through the hut,
but the door still holds.

"Both of us!" she says and I move along so that there's
room for us both to get a purchase on the floorboard and
lift.

CREEEAK!

The nails come free, one by one, along the bending
floorboard until—

WHACK!

The door is starting to splinter apart around the hinges.

"One more lift!" I say and we stand and the board pulls
back to create a bigger gap. The dark space below is just
high enough from the ground to crawl through. I stick my
head through the gap and can just make out a little hatch
door in the boarded-up panels. It must be where the firewood is stored.

The girl goes first, but before I follow her, I cross the
room to open the fireplace. Struggling to control my esca-
lating fear and cringing away from the heat, I lash out with

the poker to scatter the hot logs and coals onto the floor. I pull the stove's gas bottle from the kitchen and toss it onto the hot pile. A time-delay bomb.

I squeeze down through the hole in the floor, and together we crawl and slide our way to the hatch door. It won't budge.

"We're snowed in!" she says.

"Not for long!" I say, kicking the door off its hinges. Then, I start clawing at the snow to tunnel out.

Above us, the house creaks and cracks under attack.

The tunnel before us soon slopes up, and we climb and burrow our way upwards to breach the surface a metre above. Behind us, the door of the cabin shatters down to the floor.

"Argh!" I exclaim as I pull the girl out of the hole and we run blindly through the freezing darkness.

KLAP-BOOM!

The explosion of the gas tank rips through the still night. A split second later there is a second blast, created from the furious force of the compressed gas in the wooden hut. Flames shoot up and out, and for a moment, the world around us is as bright as day. As burning chunks of the cabin rain down around us, I can see the tall, black shimmering silhouette against the light.

I hear the terrifying howl of the wolf pack.

I see eyes through the darkness, close to me. Unflinching, reflecting the flickering light of the fire, they burn into my very being. I'm trying to fight, trying to run, but in the end, all I can feel is—

Despair.

SAM

"Ah, you're awake," a man in a white coat said to Sam. "How are you feeling?"

"OK, I guess . . ." Sam said, sitting up a little in bed.

"Take it easy there," the man said, standing close to Sam's side. "You've been through quite a lot."

"Where am I? Who are you?"

"You're at the Academy's London campus," the man said. "I'm one of the doctors here."

"How . . . how'd I get here?"

"Hmm," the doctor scratched his chin. "You don't recall? Maybe we could start with what you *do* remember?"

Sam was quiet and distant for a moment. "I was just dreaming," he said.

"Oh? OK. Tell me about that, then."

"A nightmare . . ." Sam looked around. There was one window, letting daylight spill into the room. "Can I speak to the Professor?"

"Of course, of course. Let's just make sure you're feeling up to having visitors first."

"I'm fine," Sam said. "I'm tired, that's all. And a bit dizzy."

"Then perhaps you should get a little more rest. Try to sleep."

"OK." Sam shook his head slightly, trying to clear it of the grogginess. The doctor passed him a drink. It was orange and fizzy, and Sam gulped it down gratefully.

He thought about the day ahead, and the week ahead. All that he had to do.

The next Dreamer—I saw her. Her name is Nika. Where were we . . . ?

"We've got so much to do," Sam frowned, frustrated at his own confusion.

"What are you thinking?" the doctor asked.

"I'm . . . I'm not exactly sure."

"Break it down," the doctor said, his voice kind and soothing. "Start at the very beginning."

"Of what I remember?"

"Yes, Sam, that may help with your amnesia. Why don't you tell me about being a Dreamer—one of the last 13?"

"OK . . ." Sam focused on the answer. "Well, there are thirteen Dreamers. And it's my job to find them all. Seven, including me, have been found. I'm still searching for the last six. The next one, I now know—her name is Nika."

"Nika," the doctor repeated, scribbling again on his clipboard. "What can you tell me about her?"

"She's . . . somewhere cold. There was snow on the ground. If I don't find Nika, and the rest of them, before the others do, then this race will be over."

"Tell me what you remember of the others."

"Gabriella was the first Dreamer I found, in Italy. Then Xavier, my old school friend. Zara, I met in Paris. Everything was fine each time until Solaris . . ."

"Solaris?" the doctor said, as though the name meant nothing to him. "And he is . . . ?"

Sam forced himself to sit up. "Don't you know? How could you not know?" he asked.

Something's not right.

"Sam, I'm trying to medically assess you," the doctor explained, "I need to know what *you* know."

"Oh, right. Well, he's evil. He haunts our nightmares—all of the last 13 Dreamers—and he haunts us in real life too. He wants the Gears that we see in our dreams. Well, he wants to assemble the Bakhu machine himself, to use it to win the race by finding the Dream Gate. But he wants to use whatever is beyond the Gate to plunge the world into an age of nightmares and darkness."

"Very good, Sam. Go on."

"Solaris took the Gears from us in Germany and Paris. And then they tried to rob us, but we fought back."

"They?" the doctor asked, adding to his notes.

"Mac—and Hans. They tried to take the Gears I found with the other Dreamers, Rapha and Maria. They're the Dreamers from Brazil and Cuba. But we managed to keep those Gears." Sam smiled at the memory.

"Excellent."

"Yep. But then it fell apart. Number seven, Cody." Sam spat out the name, anger rising in his voice.

"Cody?"

"From the US. He lied to me. He and his parents sold me out to Mac. Took me to Bureau 13 in Denver."

"What happened there?"

"Solaris," Sam whispered. He leaned back and looked up at the ceiling. "Mac set up a fake nuclear emergency. But he died. I escaped from Solaris, I didn't know where I was heading . . . I can't remember after that . . . how I got here exactly."

"What happened to Cody, Sam?" the doctor asked.

"I don't know. They got in an escape pod, like me."

"And the Gears?" the doctor said.

"I'm trying to remember," Sam said. "All the Gears were taken from me—the ones from Brazil, Cuba and the Grand Canyon. But then Solaris gave them back to me. He said we needed to stick together. I couldn't believe it. I don't understand what he's doing . . ."

"And this nightmare you've just had?"

"There was a fire. There's always fire—in my nightmares I mean. And him . . ." Sam closed his eyes, before adding, "Sorry, I have a headache. I feel sleepy."

The doctor nodded and pressed a button by Sam's bed. A few seconds later, a nurse entered. They talked in hushed tones, then she came over and injected a clear liquid into the IV tube in Sam's arm.

"This will help you get some rest," the doctor said. "Then we can talk again."

Before Sam could say another word—he was out.

"Sam?"

Sam opened his eyes. Doctors in white coats and masks looked down at him, backlit by blindingly bright light.

"He's awake."

"Where . . ." Sam said, his mouth dry, "where am I?"

"Up the dosage," one of the men said.

Sam turned his head and tried to look around the room. He thought he counted at least six people, but couldn't be sure. The constant bleeping of machines rang in his ears.

"Where am I?" he asked again.

No one answered. Before Sam could say another word, he was back floating in the warm sea of a deep sleep.

ALEX

"Really?" Alex said, looking around the dark, musty basement.

"It's been owned by the Dreamer Council for almost a century," Shiva said. He tried a light switch, but nothing happened. "But mothballed in recent years—locked up and left alone."

They were in a derelict building in downtown Manhattan. The basement was a cavernous void with towering ceilings and a row of skinny windows at the top, through which Alex could see pedestrians' feet and the tops of buildings across the street. Other than that, inside all he could see was inky darkness and strange shadows cast by the light from their flashlights.

"Did they forget to pay the power bill?" Alex quipped.

"No one's been down here for a decade," Shiva replied. "Here, hold my light for a sec."

Alex took Shiva's flashlight, shining both lights onto the fuse box for Shiva to inspect.

"Ten years?" Alex said. "So why are we here now?"

"Because," Shiva said, pulling out old-fashioned fuses and

checking their condition, "this is linked to the Washington Monument."

"Accessing the Dreamscape?"

"Yeah. Simliar tech, only this is *slightly* more modern." Shiva rattled a fuse by his ear, looked at it closely, then put it back. "Anyway, unlike the systems at the Eiffel Tower, they haven't turned on any of this stuff down here since Jedi's arrival. He modernized everything for the Academy and Council. The last time anyone was here was probably to deal with the rat problem."

"Rat problem?" Alex said, checking around his feet.

"Relax, I'm kidding!" Shiva said. "Aha, found it."

Alex watched as the Enterprise's computer and tech genius rewired a blown fuse and placed it back into position.

"And then—" Shiva flicked the switch again and bank after bank of lights overhead flashed on "—there was light!"

A couple of large light bulbs blew, one sending down a shower of sparks.

"Bound to happen," Shiva said. "Not to worry."

Alex saw sheets covering what looked like massive metal totem poles arranged in the centre of the room.

"And they are?"

"This basement holds a collection of Tesla's inventions that the Council salvaged over the years," Shiva explained. "This place functioned as his secondary workshop. A place to hide all his Dreamer tech which he didn't want investors in his wireless energy experiments to know about."

He walked over to the nearest poles and gave the covering sheets a heavy tug, causing them to slither to the floor in a cloud of dust. Shiva doubled over coughing. "Guess I . . . should . . . have stood farther . . . back!"

Alex wasn't listening.

Wow. I'm standing right in the middle of the history of the modern world.

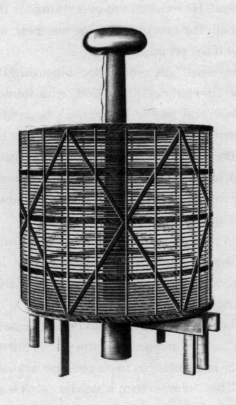

"Are these what I think they are?" he stammered.

"If you're thinking they're original Tesla coils, then yes," Shiva said, finally straightening up and coming over to stand with Alex next to a coil. "Magnificent, aren't they?"

Alex reached out to touch the coil, running his hands over the metal wires. "This is amazing! To think Tesla actually made these himself," he said.

"I think he probably had some assistants helping out, but I take your point and I am encouraged by your apparent awe. Now I need you to be *my* assistant. Come with me."

Alex followed Shiva down the steel staircase to the basement's lower level. "I know about Tesla from science class—inventor and genius, all that," Alex said.

"He was one serious science dude," Shiva said. "Come on, help me take a look through what we've got that still works down here."

SAM'S DREAM

I wake up in a room. The same white one as before, but it's not lit by bright surgical lights anymore. There is no bleeping of machines monitoring my heart rate and blood pressure. I sit up and call out. "Hello?"

Out of bed, I go to the door.

Everything looks new, but familiar in some way . . .

Déjà vu.

I am in the medical bay of the Academy's Swiss campus. I smile and open the door.

Outside, the hallway is dark but there's light at the stairs that lead upward. I walk toward them, my bare feet slapping on the polished stone floor.

Up the stairs, I am in the auditorium. There's a figure standing by the window, tall, his back to me, looking out across the snow-covered mountains.

"Professor?"

He turns around.

"Sam," he says and smiles. "Glad to see you. We have much to discuss."

I join him by the window and look out at the rocky grey

mountains covered in white snow and the grey sky. All strangely drained of colour.

"I need to know what happened to you in Denver," the Professor says.

"Solaris happened," I say. "He was there."

"And how did you get out?"

I concentrate. There is a block—a gap in my memory.

"I can't remember."

The Professor is silent for a moment. "What is the last thing you do remember?" he asks.

"The countdown," I say. "A digital countdown clock. Then I woke up someplace bright. Here, I think."

"That's it?"

"That's it."

"He needs more time."

"Sorry?"

"I said, perhaps you need more time."

"Maybe."

I shake my head, confused. "How did I get here?"

The Professor doesn't answer, and when I turn to look at him—he's gone.

"Professor?"

The room is completely empty.

I look back out the window. A snowstorm has blown in, a complete whiteout.

I cup my hands around my eyes and hold them to the glass, creating a little tunnel, trying to peer out.

There is movement. There is a figure, out there in the white. Floating in space where it doesn't belong.

Wearing orange—it's someone in an orange snow suit.

As I lean forward, I fall through the window. It hasn't broken—it has disappeared.

I look back and the Academy building is gone. The mountains are gone. The snow remains—snow, and a forest.

What's going on?

I turn to see the figure running at me. In the background I can make out the little wooden cabin in the woods.

The figure is familiar.

A dream . . . I'm in a dream.

"Nika?" I call out.

It's too late. Whoever it is, whatever is happening, is taken over by the explosion at the cabin. It's like a bomb detonating in slow motion, and the fire radiates out and consumes us both in the blink of an eye.

SAM

SLAP!

"Huh?"

"Quick!" the girl said, slapping Sam's face again. "Wake up! I have to get you out of here!"

Sam blinked away the fog of the dream. He looked around, the world around him still hazy.

A teenage girl dressed in a nurse's uniform in front of him came into focus. Her dark red hair was pulled back into a severe top knot. She was staring at him, her face worried.

She looks familiar.

Déjà vu.

"Great, I'm still dreaming . . ."

SLAP!

"Ow! OK, OK, I'm awake!"

Sam watched the girl as she began to undo the straps that were holding his arms and legs down tight against the bed frame. Her hands moved quickly, frantically even.

Is it her?

"Nika?"

She paused and looked at him, shocked for a moment, then finished undoing the last of the leather straps.

"Yes, but no . . . my real name is Arianna. I am here to rescue you, Sam. Come with me, I will explain everything later."

Arianna?

"But you know me?" Sam said. He got to his feet groggily as she helped him get upright.

"No, I know who you *are*. Quick! We must hurry."

"What's wrong with me?" Sam said, still trying to find his balance.

"They drugged you, so that you would sleep and dream as much as possible."

"The Academy drugged me?" Sam asked, confused.

"No. It was the people who we do not want to find us breaking out of here," Arianna said. "They want to harvest all that you see in your dreams." She pulled a flask from her backpack, took off the cap and offered it to Sam. "Quick, drink this."

"What is it?"

"It will help to flush out the drug they gave you."

Sam hesitantly sipped from the metal flask. It tasted of lemons and was slightly fizzy. Arianna tilted it to his lips again, forcing him to gulp it down.

Sam drank almost the whole flask and then wiped his mouth, nodding. "Thanks," he managed to get out and then—

He doubled over and vomited onto the floor.

"Sorry," he said, once it was over. "That was gross."

"That's the reaction that I hoped for, to help clear out your system," Arianna said.

"You *knew* that would happen?" Sam asked, shaking his head.

Arianna ignored his question and thrust a set of clothes at him. "Put these on."

He pulled them on, discarding his hospital gown. "What about my Stealth Suit?"

"And this," she said, ignoring him again and handing him a small device shaped like a hearing aid. "It will translate Russian to English for you."

"Russian?" Sam paused. "I'm in *Russia?*"

"Yes. We need to break out of this security compound—now. If they find me, I will be 'disappeared,' forever this time."

"So that doctor . . ." Sam said, understanding slowly dawning on him.

So I wasn't dreaming about him? But how'd I get to Russia?

He put the earpiece neatly inside his ear. Arianna said a few words that meant nothing to him, until she leaned close and adjusted a tiny dial. In one ear, he could hear her Russian phrases. In the other ear through the tiny device—

"Testing, testing." A crystal clear English translation came through the earpiece. "Can you understand me?"

"Got it. Wow," Sam said, signalling with a thumbs up. "So how do I know this isn't the dream and that was real?"

Arianna raised her hand to his face.

"Alright! I take your point. I'm awake—and somehow in Russia."

"We must leave now," she said, pulling Sam's arm over her shoulders to support him as they walked. Her slender frame belied the strength in her muscled body as she took his weight.

Is she an athlete?

"The reinforcements will be here soon," she said.

"Reinforcements?"

"They set off an alarm before I could stop them."

"Who are the reinforcements?" Sam repeated his question.

"Sam," she said, looking at him. "You must trust me, OK? I'll explain everything."

Sam looked into her blue eyes, already familiar, as they pleaded for his cooperation.

This Dreamer really is on our side. I know it.

"OK," he said. "I trust you."

EVA

"It's like they've forgotten Sam already," Eva said to Lora, as she watched staff positioning banners announcing some kind of inter-school competition.

How can they be doing sports competitions at a time like this?

"They haven't forgotten him," Lora replied. "Don't ever think that."

"It's been a whole week since we got back from the US," Eva said, looking at Lora and seeing sadness in her eyes too. "A week since Sam was last seen."

"I know," Lora said. "But he's . . . Sam's OK, Eva, I'm sure of it—don't for a second believe any of those rumours that he was trapped in Denver, because he's not dead."

"You can't know that for sure." Eva thought back to the news reports she'd seen, running daily across the TV news bulletins, on the net and in the papers, of the aftermath of the emergency evacuation in Denver. Nowhere did it mention secret bases or any survivors miraculously found underground.

"I feel it," Lora said. "And you do too, in your dreams, don't you?"

Eva nodded.

"Trust that. He got out and we'll find him. It'll be alright."

"Why can't we go back there and look for him ourselves?" Eva said.

"It's still being reported as a low-level radiation leak from a plane carrying dangerous cargo," Lora said, pointing to a tablet screen that showed a reporter at Denver International Airport. "Half the airport is still off limits, and it's not easy for us to gain access to Mac's base. Believe me, the Professor has been trying. Besides, Jedi has analyzed all the footage we can get hold of, and we know that several escape pods were launched. I think one of those would have been Sam."

"Yeah, I guess, it's just we haven't heard from him," Eva said. "Do you think he's still with the others?"

"I don't know," Lora admitted. "But we know Mac was found."

"He was?" Eva said, animated.

"I didn't want to tell you before. He didn't make it," Lora replied. "A heart attack, it seems, after Solaris set off explosives. But that doesn't mean anything for Sam."

"What about Solaris?" Eva asked. "If Sam didn't leave with Mac, could he be with Solaris? I mean, I wouldn't want him to be, but if that meant he was alive . . ."

"There's still no sign. Jedi is working to track the trajectories of the escape pods, but it's proving hard. The footage we've acquired is poor quality, and it was night when they launched. Plus, it seems the pods went in very different directions—we can't decipher a launch pattern at all. But Jedi is working to see if any UFO sightings were reported that day."

"And you really believe Sam was in one of them?" Eva asked.

"Yes. And there'll be a good reason for not getting in touch."

"OK. You're right." Eva felt a little reassured. She looked out the window at the school grounds of the Academy's campus outside London, thinking how it looked like any other old, prestigious prep school.

Only some of these students are also learning how to use their other gifts.

Right now it was lunchtime and some kids were playing cricket in the sun while a soccer game was underway in another field. Countless others sat around reading and studying while they ate their lunch.

"What more can we do?" Eva said, focusing back in the room. "What can *I* do?"

"Not much for now, I'm afraid," Lora said. "You know I'll tell you as soon as there's something to be done. But in the meantime, take comfort from the fact that many of the students you see down below have been dreaming that Sam's out there and still in the race."

"They have?" Eva was stunned.

Lora nodded.

"OK, then," said Eva, suddenly more determined, "So, we'll find him. And I need to find a way to do that."

SAM

They walked as fast as Sam could manage, out of the room and into a dark hallway.

"Where are we going?" Sam asked as they quickened the pace and started to jog down the corridor toward a rickety wooden staircase.

"Someplace safe," Arianna replied.

"Wait! I can't leave without the Gears!" Sam said, pulling Arianna to a skidding stop.

"Do you know where they are?" she asked.

"Well, no. They must have taken them from me when—"

"Then you can leave without them. You must. We waste time looking for them now, we won't make it out." Arianna shook her head defiantly.

She's right, I know she's right. But to lose three Gears!

"Come now!" she said, dragging him onward. By the time they reached the end of the corridor, Sam was running alongside Arianna. In the doorway of the last room they passed, Sam saw a pair of legs poking out—nearly tripping over them as he ran. It was the doctor who had assessed him earlier, lying still on the ground.

"You killed them?" Sam asked, momentarily pausing at the sight.

"No. They are unconscious. For a long time, I hope."

"But that doctor . . ."

"Believe me, he was no doctor," Arianna answered without breaking her stride. "At least, not one in the business of helping people. Come, keep moving, quickly."

"So who was he?" Sam asked, joining her again.

"Someone trained to get you to talk."

Sam struggled to comprehend it all, the drugs still clouding his mind and making it hard to work out what was real and what he had dreamed. They went down the stairs and entered a little foyer, Sam still needing to focus on each step. Behind a desk by the door were two security guards, unconscious, like the doctor.

"What *is* this place?" Sam asked.

Certainly no hospital . . . and certainly not the Academy.

"It is what you would call 'a front.'" Arianna stopped at the foyer doors, looking out the glass window, waiting for a break in the pedestrians and traffic outside to make an unseen getaway.

"A front?"

"A fake. You know, pretend? Your room was designed to look like a hospital room. But it is nothing of the kind."

Sam looked around—the foyer was convincing, set up as a medical centre—it looked like a typical waiting room. But it was deserted. The more detail he took in, the more

Sam felt as though he'd left his brain behind somewhere. It felt as though this was making sense, but seemed otherworldly, like he was watching things from afar rather than participating in them.

Like I'm still dreaming.

"They said——" Sam began.

"You were at the Academy."

"Yeah."

"Well, you're not, Sam. Look, out there. That's Moscow. And those guys?" Arianna pointed back at the unconscious guards. "All of this is a facility set up and run by the Hypnos."

"And who are the Hypnos?"

"They're criminals who corrupt all that is good about Dreamers. They use the dreams they steal for power and control. But recently they've been working for someone else."

"Stella?" Sam asked, taking a guess.

"I don't know, we haven't been able to find out," Arianna said. "This place is what they call a 'reading centre,'" she added. She checked the monitors on the desk, watching the footage from outside on the street to make sure that the coast was clear. Satisfied, she unhooked the surveillance hard drive and put it in her pack. "We try not to leave evidence of ourselves behind, *da*?"

This girl knows what she's doing.

"So, they bring the new ones to sites like this," she continued.

"New ones?"

"Those who are newly identified. Dreamers, yes? They assess Dreamers, process them, and then send them off to the next step in their chain, to a more secure facility in Siberia. It's happened to so many in this country. You must know there are those who want to use dreams for their own purposes."

Mac, Hans, Stella . . . even the Enterprise. Yeah, I know lots of people like that.

"Siberia . . ." he said, remembering his dream of the cabin in the snow, the forest, the wolves.

"That's a place you *never* want to see," Arianna added.

"I bet," Sam said, understanding her tone. "But who are you, Arianna, really? I mean, all the other Dreamers I've met—to some extent I've had to convince each of them of their abilities, but you already know what you are, right?"

"I did. I do," Arianna sighed. "I've known for a long time that I am a Dreamer," Arianna said, putting her backpack on and looking out the front doors again. "I have spent my life rescuing Dreamers like you from the Hypnos. There's a battle raging. I hope you are ready for your part in it."

"I am. I mean, as soon as I feel back to normal. We have a mission too, you know."

"Oh, I know," Arianna said, pulling the door open and stepping outside, Sam right behind her. "But for now, welcome to Moscow, Sam."

As they walked across the road, Sam was immediately struck by how similar it felt to being in Paris—the cobbled street and graceful old buildings around them seemed so out of step with where they had just been. They turned a corner and were confronted with half a dozen rows of traffic, surging forward at the green lights swinging overhead. Sam squinted in the harsh daylight to follow Arianna as she deftly weaved between the mass of pedestrians around them.

"You're with the Academy?" Sam asked as he caught up to her, feeling more and more alive with every stride.

"No, not the Academy," Arianna said, moving even faster now. "I am one of the Nyx. We've been locked in a battle over the Dreamscape for many generations. And if we don't hurry, we will lose *everything*."

A cold wind made Sam wish for a warm coat as they navigated the busy streets.

"So this is a battle between the Nyx and the Hypnos?" he asked.

"That is correct," Arianna said. "And I am with the Nyx." She held up her left arm as they ran down a narrow side street, flashing a small star tattooed on the underside of her wrist. The Hypnos' "reading centre" was already several blocks behind them. "We all have this as a symbol of membership. We are a group of Dreamers and friends who fight for freedom. The Hypnos want to control us—all of us. They believe that if they can get to our dreams, steal our gift, then they can be in charge."

"Of Russia?" Sam said, then did a double take as they passed a fast food outlet that looked exactly as it would back home but the sign was in another, strange-looking language.

"Russia, and then the world. Keep going, faster. We have to get off the streets."

And here was me thinking that I'd need to find her . . . explain everything to her. Not this time.

Arianna took him to the end of the short laneway and paused, looking right and left. "He's not here."

"Who?"

"Our getaway," she said, looking around frantically. "He was supposed to be here, in a car."

Sam looked around—there were plenty of cars and trucks, all lumbering along in the cool morning air, though none were parked or waiting nearby.

A whistle rang out from across the street. Arianna turned and Sam followed her gaze. A beat-up old cab was pulling up to the curb, the driver hanging out the window and waving them over.

"That's him," she said, and took Sam by the arm and together they crossed the main road, dodging between honking horns. They climbed into the back seat of the taxi as the driver hit the gas and took off in a squeal of rubber against road.

"Sam, this is our friend, Boris," Arianna said. "Boris, this is our Dreamer, Sam."

Boris was huge—a giant of a man. Even squashed into the front seat, Sam could tell he was maybe two metres tall and a metre wide in the shoulders. His meaty face broke into a huge grin and he raised his fist to Sam in a gruff greeting.

"Better buckle up," Boris said, Sam simultaneously

hearing both the spoken Russian and the English translation through his earpiece.

Wow, that's going to take some getting used to.

Sam quickly followed his instructions.

He watched as Boris' eyes shifted nervously from
the road ahead to the rear-view mirror and out his side
windows. Arianna asked him something in Russian, too
quick or too quiet for Sam's earpiece to pick up. Boris
nodded and they both began looking all around, scanning
the streets.

"What is it?" Sam asked. "Trouble?"

"Cops," Arianna said. "They're close by."

"Police is bad?" Sam said. "Can't they help us?"

"Not in Russia—it's not that simple," Arianna said.

Their cab practically flew down the street, Boris' heavy
foot planted hard, the horns of other cars a loud soundtrack
to their high-speed getaway.

"Why?" Sam asked.

"Many of the police in this city are . . . *connected* to the
Hypnos," Arianna replied in Russian so Boris could follow
the conversation. "Not all of them, of course. There are
some very good cops in town, like Boris here."

Sam caught Boris smiling in the front seat.

"It has become hard to tell who you can trust anymore,
as the Hypnos are everywhere," Arianna went on, the two of
them sliding around in the back seat as Boris took a hand-
brake turn through a wide intersection. "Most of those in

power, most of those who are wealthy, have gotten to their positions by many, many years of stealing and controlling dreams. It has been a battle raging for too long, but I feel, I *know*, that it will be coming to a close, very soon. One way or another."

She stared at Sam meaningfully, a fierce intensity in her eyes.

10

ALEX

"OK," Alex said, dusting off workbenches that seemed to be covered more with dust and cobwebs than anything of use to them, "I admit that I may have skimmed over my lack of knowledge of Tesla before. Here's what I do know—old dude, dead now, inventor. Was into electricity, lived and worked here in New York for a bit. That's about it. I mean, apart from now knowing he was a Dreamer and into the Dreamscape stuff."

"Ha!" Shiva replied with a chuckle, untangling electrical cables. "Never would have guessed your limited smarts on such an important subject."

"What was that?!" Alex cried out and jumped up on a desk.

"What?"

"I saw a snake!"

"That was a bit of electrical cable," Shiva said, laughing. "Really, I thought you were a tough guy, out to save the world and all that. What happened with that?"

"I am," Alex replied, climbing back down to the floor with a nervous glance. "I'm just not crazy about snakes is all."

"You Americans," Shiva replied, still chuckling. "The city where I am from, in Bangalore, has more than snakes to worry about. This city too, I'm sure."

"Yeah, it's just . . ." Alex looked around uneasy. "I think it's their eyes and tongues that freak me out."

"Maybe you just had a bad dream about them once."

"Ha, yeah, maybe."

"Let's take five," Shiva said, tossing Alex a drink from his pack. The pair sat on ancient office chairs that squeaked and creaked under their weight.

"Weren't you ever scared of anything?" Alex asked.

"Getting caught," Shiva replied.

"By who?"

"Whoever I was hacking." He smiled.

"Nice. Do much hacking these days?"

"A little bit, for the Enterprise. Don't want to get rusty."

"Is that how you started out for them?" Alex asked.

"Yep," Shiva said. "I was hacking bank accounts that were being used by Dreamers who make their living on the wrong side of the law. While I was fooling around in a bank's database, I got caught."

"By the cops?"

"Nope. Matrix."

"Oh," Alex said. "Was he always an annoying butthead?"

"Pretty much, yep," Shiva said.

"How'd he catch you?"

"Well, he caught wind of what I was doing and then

watched me, testing me. He wanted to see if I could get around in networks undetected. Turns out I can't—least not from him. He's very, very good." Shiva broke out a packet of mixed nuts.

"Where do you think he is now?" Alex asked through a mouthful.

"With Stella someplace, doing her online dirty work."

"What would you do if you met him again?"

Shiva smiled. "What, like revenge?"

"I guess."

"I don't want to punch him in the face or anything like that. I'm too much of a pacifist." Shiva was silent for a while. Alex could practically hear him running the revenge possibilities through his mind. "I'd love to bump into him on the net again. Take him down that way, once and for all. That's how you hurt the best hackers, especially someone like Matrix."

"By beating them at their own game?"

"You know it." Shiva tossed an almond up into the air and caught it in his mouth.

"Wish I was good at something like that."

"Like catching nuts?"

"No, like you, with your hacking."

"You're pretty good with tech and computers."

"I can fix stuff. Do basic coding. Get into networks that have their backdoors left open. But that's it." Alex sighed.

"It's more than most."

"Can you show me? Teach me, I mean."

"Hacking skills?" Shiva raised an eyebrow.

Alex nodded.

"Sure." Shiva got up and stretched out his back. "But first we gotta try and get this system online. Come on, let's rock it. Oh, and mind that snake."

"Argh!" Alex jumped.

"Made you look."

"Ha, funny, just you wait, oh Great Shiva, just you wait."

"Whatever you say, Thor."

Alex tossed two nuts in the air, a second apart, and caught each in unison. Shiva's mouth dropped open in mock surprise.

"That's right," Alex said. "I got skills."

"You really had no idea that your mother was an Enterprise Agent?" Shiva said as they shifted one of the huge Tesla coils on its platform.

"Nope," Alex replied.

"Wow," Shiva said. "Phoebe's either really, really good at deception, or you're a little, you know . . ."

"Slow?"

"I was going to say thick."

"Fair enough. I'll take that."

"Really?" Shiva was taken aback.

"Sure. I can't believe it myself. I always thought my mom had the most boring job in the world, working for the Transport Department, planning new roads and analyzing traffic patterns."

"And meanwhile," Shiva said, "she was the second-in-command of a secret organization working with people whose dreams come true."

"Yep."

"Super-mom, huh?" Shiva said.

"If you say so," Alex said, standing back and admiring their work. They'd finished sorting cables and equipment that had not been touched in years, clearing enough room to work. "OK, what's next?"

"Next, we check in to the Enterprise and report on what we've found."

"What *have* we found?" Alex said, looking around. "A mess? Dust? Where all the world's old power cables went to die?"

"No," Shiva said, rapping his knuckles on one of the three Tesla coils. "We've found a way to home in on Matrix's location."

11

SAM

Sam struggled to hold Arianna's gaze.

Is she talking about the race? The fate of the whole world really does depend on this . . .

"You think I can help bring Dreamers freedom here?" Sam said. "Is that why you rescued me?"

"Yes. These days the Hypnos are everywhere. They are too strong for the Academy and even the Enterprise. They've become increasingly bold, operating in the open."

"But you still don't know who their leader is?"

"We never even knew they had one, until recently. I heard rumours of one man, but I think he has a boss too. The boss is very good at staying in the background. There are rumours that he is a very rich and powerful man, with connections all over the planet. Somehow able to wield influence over even the senior Hypnos who have always been here running the country."

"Great, more bad guys in the shadows . . ." Sam said, looking out the grimy window of the cab. A flash of a scene from Denver ran through his mind—of Mac lying unconscious, and of Solaris.

"Sometimes," Arianna said, "those who join the Hypnos just need a little money for their family, they feel they have no choice but to betray their own. That's why the Nyx exist, why it has always existed—to protect Dreamers."

"So why do you need me? I'm supposed to get *your* help."

"Don't you see, Sam?" Arianna said. "You, the last 13, the Academy and Enterprise, us. This war is global, and we are all ready and willing to fight together. Right, Boris?"

"Yes! Fight! Win!" Boris exclaimed loudly in English.

Sam sensed Boris relaxing a little as they merged onto a road that was fairly clear of traffic. Up ahead were several main turnoffs, with signs for highways out of the city.

"So how'd I get here? In Moscow, I mean, to the Hypnos facility?"

"You were found in a pod that splashed down in the Black Sea. The force of the landing probably knocked you unconscious. The Russian Navy retrieved you. Routine DNA tests would have been done to confirm if you were a powerful Dreamer, and then you were transferred to the Hypnos reading centre for monitoring. That's where they take everyone at first."

"And then what?"

"Well, they start by questioning you, getting all your memories and also monitoring your dreams. Then they'd move on to stage two."

"What's stage two?"

"Harvesting DNA—mapping it and mining it for

information that will increase their hold on power. Of course, since they realized they had Sam, the first of the last 13 . . . who knows what they had planned for *you*."

"Oh man," Sam sighed.

"Man?" Arianna looked confused.

"Yeah, it means, like, yikes, whoa . . . um, shivers, that kind of thing."

"Shivers," Boris said over his shoulder. "You cold? Want heater put on?"

"No," Sam said, breaking into a smile. "I mean, ah, it doesn't matter. But you mentioned DNA harvesting—that sounds, geez, I don't even know . . ."

"It's bad, very bad," Arianna said. "Sometimes, the subject does not survive."

Sam looked out his window, watching the Moscow traffic. "When was this?"

"When was what?" Arianna asked.

"When did I land in the Black Sea?"

"Tuesday."

"What day is it today?" Sam said.

"Wednesday," Arianna replied.

"OK, so only yesterday? They can't have monitored too many of my dreams in only one day."

"No . . . it was Tuesday last week."

"Last week!" Sam was genuinely shocked. "I was held there for over a week?"

Arianna nodded. "It took us some time to organize the

rescue. We tried to move as quickly as we could, especially once we knew who you were. We had to get you out before the Hypnos could use that to their advantage."

"I'm very grateful—to you and Boris . . . the Academy and Enterprise would never have found me there in time. Speaking of, I need to let my friends know I'm OK. I'm worried about some of them too, it'd be good to know they're alright."

"We will contact them, once we are safe."

"Hang on!" Boris yelled as he slammed on the brakes and came to a sudden stop to avoid colliding with the car in front. Directly ahead was a massive truck, jack-knifed at an intersection. No traffic was getting through the accident site at all. Boris threw the taxi into reverse and looked over his shoulder as he made a U-turn. "New plan—I will have to go another way."

"Head for the backstreets," Arianna said and he nodded and stepped on the gas. Behind them, the blue flashing lights of black, unmarked police cars were arriving on the scene. "And hurry!"

12

"I think we're OK," Sam said. He looked out the back window and couldn't see any police cars following them. The sun occasionally broke through the grey clouds. With every passing minute the traffic seemed to increase.

"We're not OK yet," Arianna said. "Until we're off the roads and out of sight, I won't feel safe."

Sam turned to look out the side window.

"Where are we?"

"Still in Moscow."

Sam nodded, watching the world out the window. "So that 'doctor' back at the centre, would he have been high up in the Hypnos?"

Arianna was silent, then Boris swore in Russian under his breath, too quietly for Sam's earpiece to work.

"What's wrong?" Sam asked her.

"That man, Demetri, has something of a brutal reputation," she said. "Boris would have liked to have met him."

Boris' huge grin in the rear-view mirror suggested to Sam that it would not have been a fun meeting for Demetri.

He touched the brakes and swerved sharply to weave through the cars on the congested road. "Only one thing worse than the Hypnos—Moscow traffic," he muttered.

"Where are we going, for help?" Sam said.

"The Kremlin."

"Isn't that where the Russian government and the President are?"

"Yes."

"So, from what you said before, I'm guessing there will be Hypnos there too?"

"Yes. Without a doubt."

"We're going into the dragon's den . . ." Sam said. He watched as Boris made bold driving manoeuvres through traffic, turning down a narrow alley before merging onto a busy main road again.

Loud honks and furious gestures followed them but Boris just smiled and waved in response.

"How did you get involved in all this anyway?" Sam said, tearing his eyes away from the crammed streets.

"My adoptive parents," Arianna answered. "Their families have been members of the Nyx for generations. They told me everything—that's how it's been for centuries."

"So you've known you were a Dreamer for a few years?"

Arianna nodded.

"And you knew what it meant when you dreamed of me?"

"I didn't dream of you, Sam. Boris did," she replied, ever watchful of the other vehicles around them.

"Boris? But we need to follow *your* dream," Sam said, "to find the Gear."

Arianna stared at him, but said nothing.

"I dreamed of you. You are the next of the last 13," Sam explained. "I thought you knew of the prophecy? It's the only way—my dream leads me to the others, and your dreams show us where to find the Gears for the Bakhu machine."

"So it *is* true," Arianna sighed. "Somehow I knew but . . ." she paused. "I'm afraid I have some bad news."

"What?" Sam said, suddenly feeling panicked.

Before she could answer, Boris swore loudly in Russian and the car accelerated so quickly, Arianna and Sam were thrown back into their seats. They looked out the rear window to see two cop cars, blue flashing lights blazing, a few hundred metres back and closing fast.

"I'm sorry to tell you, Sam," Arianna said, "but I can't dream anymore."

13

EVA

"The Four Corners Competition," said Xavier, glancing up from reading about the Academy's history, "more commonly known as 'the Dreamer Doors,' is held each year to determine which Dreamers are best at steering dreams. To paraphrase what I've just read here."

"You don't paraphrase in good English," Gabriella said.

"Good point, my learned Italian friend . . ." Xavier said.

Eva rolled her eyes.

"So here it says there are preliminary heats, which are dreaming challenges," Xavier went on. "The result of these challenges decides the team of three that will represent each school in the international competition."

Eva sat with Xavier, Zara, Maria, Gabriella and Rapha, in the school café, silent, taking it all in. Gabriella, Eva noticed, had been arguing with Xavier ever since they'd met, the pop star never giving in.

"I wonder why they do not cancel it this year," Gabriella said, "because of what's happening with us, with the race."

Eva had to admit, that made some sense.

Sam's missing, Cody betrayed us, the last three Gears are

lost. The hunt for the 13 and the Dream Gate, it all seems too hard.

"Why have a silly competition like this at all?" Eva said. "We should be doing everything we can to find Sam."

"It might be to take the students' minds from this," Zara said. "They are sad, no?"

The group digested this thought for a moment, then Rapha said, "Yes, I believe it. They are sad, and worried, angry—about what happened in Switzerland, the Council, the betrayals of your Guardians and . . ."

Eva nodded and stared out the window.

"That may all well be true, but *I* heard Lora say that they were going ahead with this Doors thing to help with the race *and* Sam," Xavier said.

"Really?" Eva said, surprised. "If that's true, then that's—that's awesome!"

"Here, look at this," Xavier said, and he held up his tablet. "This is a picture of the world as governed by the Dreamer Council."

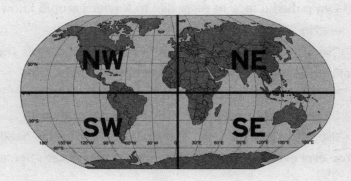

"Basically," he went on, "it's divided through the zero longitude and latitude lines, with the schools in each quadrant competing first against each other, then in a World Cup-type final."

"Which quadrant do we fall in?" Maria asked.

"We're just west of Greenwich, or the Prime Meridian," Xavier said, scrolling through the information, "so we're part of the North-West, which encompasses North America too. North-East has their main Academy in Shanghai. South-West is in Sao Paulo in Brazil—"

"Really?" Rapha said, the Brazilian Dreamer clearly surprised that he'd had an Academy in his own backyard.

"Says so here," Xavier replied. "And the South-East is in Johannesburg."

"Cool," Zara said.

"And each quadrant has a Dreamer Academy like this one?" Eva asked.

"Apparently," Xavier said. "Some have more than one. You haven't read about all this yet?"

Eva pulled a face in response to Xavier's stupid know-it-all grin.

"So it's like the World Cup," Gabriella said. "All the nations get the chance to compete against each other."

"What, like the soccer World Cup?" Xavier replied.

"Football," Gabriella said. "The *Football* World Cup."

"Soccer is not football," Xavier said, shaking his head. "You ever even watched an NFL game? That sucker's fierce.

That's football. Huge guys running into each other. None of this running around to score what, like one goal per game?"

"Do you watch rugby?" Zara asked him.

"Never heard of it," Xavier replied.

"You're talking of your silly game where your players run around in tights and helmets?" Gabriella laughed. "Besides, with *real football*, it is not a game."

"Neither is this . . ." Eva said, preparing to give them a rundown of what she was reading. "It says here that each year, thirteen Dreamers compete in the Dreamer Doors, three from each Academy, plus the leader of the previous winning team who is known as the Steerer. It's that person's dream that the rest are competing in. It seems as though the North-East Academy currently holds the title and have done for the past six years. Each group of three will have a team challenge, as well as competing for an overall individual award."

"This list of individual winners includes Tobias and Lora," Xavier said, reading in close to Eva. "And here," he pointed down at another name, "Sebastian McPherson—isn't that the Professor's name? Was that his son?"

Eva nodded.

"What was he like?" Gabriella asked.

"Sebastian?" Eva said. "I barely knew him. I just met him once or twice. But he was . . . he was cold, a bit mean, but then I guess he was just serious—he knew as well as anyone the importance of the race. Definitely very focused and determined. And it looks like he was smart too—it says here he's the only student in the comp's history to have won twice."

"Sebastian must have been a boss Dreamer," Xavier said.

"It wouldn't surprise me," Eva said. "He did have that odd air of brilliance about him."

"But hold on, I thought only seniors could enter it?" Maria said.

"No," Eva replied, "it's based on your dreams, not your age. Selection occurs via a dream challenge before the tournament. Anyone who wants to take part can enter, and whichever students are given the highest scores go on to represent their school in the competition."

"So not very easy to prepare for it," Rapha said.

"If you can dream, then I guess you're as ready as you are going to be," Maria said. "Right?"

A final silence descended upon the group, and Eva couldn't help think of how things would have been if Sam had been there.

He'd have won this for sure.

14

SAM

"You can't dream?" Sam said, shocked. In the back of the cab, he bumped around as Boris sped through more back streets to get around the horrendous traffic. "But that *can't* be . . . you *have* to dream."

"Believe it," Arianna replied, watching out her window, sadness in her voice. "Not since I was sent to that place in Siberia."

"You've been there?" Sam said.

"Yes, when I was twelve. It is there that they take away your dreams."

"They steal your dreams?"

"Yes—and erase them."

"How?"

"An implant," she said as she put a finger to her head. "Like a computer chip. And I can't get it out. They've done it to thousands of us over the years. And we've tried to get them out, believe me."

"Why would they do that?"

"To take our dreams. To make it so that we are not a threat to their power."

"But—but what if maybe you still dream but *they* are seeing it instead of you?"

Arianna looked at him thoughtfully. "Very well understood, Sam. Yes, we have discovered that they are doing such things, using our dreams for their own gain."

"Then it could be you've had the dream about where the next Gear is," Sam said with dread. "And maybe someone connected to the Hypnos has watched the dream, or at least recorded it."

"Perhaps . . ." she seemed to think about it. "Probably."

"Then we have to get there—to Siberia, if that's where their main headquarters are!"

She nodded, then lurched forward as their car was rammed from behind.

A police sedan had smashed into their rear bumper, and Boris reacted by slamming on the brakes.

Both cars came to a screeching halt.

He looked over his shoulder and smiled at the cops as they got out of their car, reaching for their pistols—

"Hold on!" Arianna said as Boris flipped a switch on the dashboard.

VROOOM!

Sam was thrown hard into the seat as their taxi surged forward as though under rocket power—which seemed to be the only explanation for the way they shot down the street in a matter of seconds. Boris hit the brakes and took them screeching around a bend, then swung the wheel the other way to make a sharp right turn, crossing several lanes of traffic to honking horns and yells from drivers. Ahead, they were headed toward a massive wall.

"Get us to safety!" Arianna shouted to Boris in Russian.

For his part, Boris drove like a stunt-car driver.

"What *is* this car?" Sam said. "A rocket?"

"It has some modifications that Boris added on," Arianna replied, like it was all in a day's work for her. "This might look like an old car, but it is as fast as anything else in the city."

"Great," Sam said, fighting the G-forces of a curve on the road. "We're going to break the sound barrier in a taxi cab."

"No," Arianna said, pointing to a vast brick-walled compound. "We are going to break into that."

15

ALEX

"**T**esla really invented this stuff a hundred years ago?" Alex said.

"Yep," Shiva replied.

"Genius."

"That and more."

"Genius *and* Dreamer."

"And that's probably just the half of it."

Alex took the wrench from Shiva and passed him a screwdriver. "And we're trying to get all this online now because . . ."

"Because the rules have changed," Shiva replied, screwing back on an inspection plate on the last coil. "Since the government shut down its original Dreamer program in the 1950s and the Enterprise took its place, they have been constrained by a ton of rules."

"Such as not tapping into everyone's dreams and sucking them up and storing them away some place?"

"Exactly. Which is all well and good, in theory."

"Go on," Alex urged.

"Tesla never got this system to work beyond a small

section of Manhattan," Shiva said, using a rag to wipe grease from his hands. "He never had the power he needed."

"Which is why you brought in those extra power cables from the building upstairs?"

"Yep. The power will be boosted a thousand times compared to what was available to Tesla. It'll give us a good idea of what these first coils can do. Pass me that other screwdriver."

"And if it all works as Tesla thought," Alex said, passing the tool over, "how far will the range be?"

"These coils, with this power? City wide, easy."

"Wow!"

"Yeah, well," Shiva put in the last screw and tossed the driver into the toolbox and got to his feet, "if we had a lot of power, like, a whole power station, and bigger coils than these, the range, theoretically, would be total."

"Total?"

"Worldwide."

"That's incredible!" Alex looked at the tall Tesla dream coils with new-found respect. "We could see into *everyone's* dreams . . ."

"A power that comes with a lot of responsibility. That's part of why the government shut the program down. I mean, imagine if we could see every thought, every secret in people's dreams?"

"That could be cool. No more wars, maybe? Crime

rates would fall—police could stop criminals before they commit a crime."

"Or it might *start* wars. Or they might arrest people just for dreaming of criminal activity," Shiva said.

"Oh." Alex's brow furrowed.

"It's a slippery slope, my friend," Shiva said, wiping the machinery grease off his hands. "You see into everyone's mind, you open doors that are hard to close."

Alex nodded. "If this works? And if we manage to switch it on—I mean, with more power," he said, "we'll see everything, every dream. We might not even need Sam."

"In a sense you're right—but we still need him to dream, and the rest of the last 13. It might just make things a whole lot easier."

"But we won't need to rely on any of the Dreamers," Alex said, the possibilities dawning on him. "Maybe we could find those working against us! And maybe we won't need to find the 13 in order to get to the Gate."

"We won't need to find them, true, but we'd still be reliant on them."

"Because we need them to dream . . . in order for us to see it," Alex said.

"Exactly," Shiva said. "Anyway, let's focus on finding Stella and Matrix. Oh, man, I hope this works!"

"Then we *have* to get this system up and running!" Alex said, standing from his seat next to a Tesla coil. He felt a buzz running up and down his spine, as though he was another Tesla totem in the room. "We can be the ones to open the Dream Gate, don't you see? We can see what lies beyond . . ."

"And be masters of the universe!" Shiva said, goading his friend on.

"You're . . . mocking me?"

"No, I think it's admirable, your sense of belief. Just don't get too carried away, will you?"

Alex was a little dumbfounded. "What do you mean?"

"There are reasons that these have been idle so long," Shiva said, tossing Alex a can of soda and popping one for himself, "beyond the, shall we say, ethical restraints."

Alex looked from his friend to the coils. "So what, some people at the Enterprise don't believe you?" Alex said. "They think that the coils won't work?"

"That's what *lots* of people think," Shiva admitted, "including our own Director. Well, pretty much everyone but me, to tell you the truth. Although I think Stella used to believe it. And maybe Matrix, but he liked the *idea* of it, not this old tech."

"Well, who cares what others think?"

Shiva laughed. "That's been a mantra of mine over the years," he said. "Besides, no one was as good with the hands-on work as I am. My dad used to be a watchmaker, see?"

He showed Alex an intricate timepiece linked by a small gold chain to his belt, then pocketed it again.

"I've been working for years studying Tesla's work," Shiva said, "and I believe, with every bone in my body, that this *will* work."

"Me too."

"Spoken like a true believer," Shiva said.

"I mean it. We could be heroes!"

"First things first, hero," Shiva said, pointing to the massive electrical cables. "We've got to attach those before we can think about having *any* power!"

SAM

SHARE THE POWER! the chant went in Russian, Sam's little earpiece picking it out from the hum of the crowd assembled in front of the towering brick wall.

From what Sam could piece together, the protest was about an upcoming election. Thousands of people were waving placards and chanting. Hundreds of police dressed in riot gear were lined up behind barricades.

"We will get out up here," Arianna said to Sam. "We get out and move fast. Follow me, no matter what."

"Where are we headed?"

"To meet a friend who will smuggle us out of the city through the tunnel system."

"Tunnels that lead all the way out of the city?" Sam asked, amazed. To him, it seemed they'd moved closer to the centre of Moscow, one of the largest cities in the world.

"*Da*," Arianna replied as Boris slowed and changed lanes, headed for a drop-off zone. "Some have been here under the city for centuries, others since the Cold War. They lead to secure sites underneath the mountains. They are safe, most are unused."

Sam nodded and tried to look unfazed but a shiver ran down his spine.

Tunnels that lead to secure sites underneath mountains . . .

He'd been through that, only a few days ago, and his life was still upside down because of it. He looked ahead at the crowd, then out the back window. Although out of sight, Sam knew the cops would be only a minute or two behind them.

"I have to contact my friends back at the Academy," Sam said.

"Not until we get somewhere they can't track phone calls too easily."

"How about an email?"

"The same," Arianna said. "Besides, with everyone in the world looking for you, perhaps it is helpful that some believe you to be dead."

Sam hadn't looked at it that way.

If you're the number one person being hunted on the planet, being "dead" does have its advantages.

"So this is the Kremlin?" Sam asked as they slowed. Boris produced ID and they were waved through the security cordon and the gates of the massive brick-walled facility—a city within a city.

"It is," Arianna said. "It is the seat of power in this country, and also the Hypnos stronghold."

"And you thought coming *here* was a good idea?" Sam checked back over his shoulder—out in the expansive square behind them, two of the cop cars came to a screeching halt. There were uniformed police and soldiers *everywhere*.

"Yes," Arianna said. "They will not chase us in here. They will not even expect us to be here, for it is a stupid move, no?"

"Ah, yeah, sounds like it," Sam said.

"We have a high-ranking friend here," she replied. "Just follow me—and whatever you do, do not say anything to anyone, you will draw too much attention."

Sam did as instructed. He watched as soldiers in immaculate uniforms marched and paraded. Small groups of tourists were being chaperoned about by minders. Big black limos were dropping off large old men who Sam guessed were politicians, bureaucrats and businessmen.

"See you outside the city," Arianna said to Boris and he drove off, leaving them alone, his bright yellow, battered taxi soon out of sight.

"We couldn't just drive away with him?" Sam asked. "Rocket our way right out of town?"

"Boris will spread the chase," Arianna said as she walked. "The Hypnos on our tail will continue to track him around the city streets. He is a cop, so he will get away if they catch him. It is us they're looking for."

Makes sense, Sam thought, then watched as his new friend spoke to a guard by a security gate who then waved them through to an empty security line. Arianna spoke to a receptionist at a security booth and the two of them waited patiently as she checked the two IDs that Arianna pulled out from her pack, then they were pointed to a building.

"What if he's not in?" Sam asked as he kept in close step next to Arianna.

"He will be," Arianna said. "He is always working."

Sam nodded. "I really *do* need to tell my friends that I made it out of Denver," he whispered to her. "To make a call, I mean, to the Academy."

A group of soldiers stopped at a tour group, looking at faces as if searching for someone, and then left without a word or any apparent recognition of Sam and Arianna as they passed.

"Yes, of course," Arianna replied. "We will use my friend's phone here. We can even have him call and say that you're OK."

"Good idea." Sam smiled. He instantly felt better at the prospect of his friends knowing what was going on. He imagined speaking to Eva, Lora and the Professor—to hear news of what had happened in his absence.

Inside the building, Arianna flashed her ID and within a minute a man in a black suit appeared behind Arianna. Sam gave a little head movement toward him, and Arianna turned—

"You are here to see Undersecretary Popov?" he said in Russian.

"Yes," Arianna replied. "It is urgent. He is expecting us."
Sam could tell that she was wary.

And defiant. Strong, in the face of authority. A good friend to have.

The man checked their IDs slowly. "Follow me," he said finally.

Arianna hesitated. "I know how to get to his office," she countered. "I have been there many times. You do not need to escort us."

"The Undersecretary is not *in* his office," the man replied. "But if you will follow me, I will take you to him."

Arianna looked to Sam, and he got the glimpse of something in her eyes that said this seemed wrong, but she turned to the guy and simply said, "OK."

They followed the suited man through a rabbit warren of hallways. Sam imagined everyone they passed was a member of the Hypnos, ready to spring into action and kidnap them.

"Be ready to follow my lead," Arianna whispered to Sam out of the corner of her mouth.

He nodded.

Ready when you are.

The guy stopped at the top of a flight of stairs, and gestured to them. "Please," he said in a friendly tone, indicating they should proceed down the stairs.

Arianna walked by, and Sam could tell that she was tense and poised for trouble.

As Sam followed, he noticed that the man had a holstered pistol under his suit jacket.

Some kind of security guy. What do I do if he reaches for the gun? Take him down? Then what? It'll be the two of us and one gun against all those soldiers and guards. Or do I let him take us captive and see what happens?

The stairs went a long way down, with old metal doors

at each landing. The way was lit by grimy old light bulbs, throwing dark shadows in the deep corners of the stairs. Sam continued to run through his options and planning jujitsu moves.

"Take the next door," the guy instructed from behind them.

Sam caught a look from Arianna. She was getting ready for something.

OK, so action it is.

He started getting ready to make a move too, settling his nerves, breathing slowly.

They stopped at the next landing. The man opened the door and motioned for them to go through. As they went in, Sam looked behind to see the guy's hand move for the pistol under his jacket—

Arianna spun around and sliced her hand hard into his neck, forcing the guy to double over. Her knee flew up with lightning speed and *WHACK!* the guy was out, unconscious, a heap on the floor.

"Nice work!" Sam said.

"Quick," she said, taking the guy's radio set and listening in to the security team's conversations. "Oh no!"

"What?"

"I hear Popov's voice."

"That's good!"

"No, Sam, it's not," she said, her face crestfallen. "He's ordering security to find us and arrest us. Popov has been compromised . . . he is our friend no more."

"Then we're on our own," Sam said.

"Yes," Arianna said, putting the radio earpiece into her ear. "We must make for the escape tunnels ourselves."

"I thought we were heading for tunnels!" Sam said. He could barely keep up as Arianna took them back up two flights of stairs.

"We are!" Arianna replied, climbing three steps at a time.

"Shouldn't tunnels be down, not up?" Sam said, looking down the gap in between the handrails to the dark void below. "Like, deep underground or something?"

"Yes," she said, stopping at the first landing they'd initially passed during their descent. "But the entrance to them is not in this wing."

"Great. So where was that guy taking us?"

"Some prison cells, by the sounds of it," Arianna replied, pointing to the little radio earpiece she wore. "Security are going berserk, calling for the guy to reply. We must be very careful."

"Careful is my middle name."

"Americans—such odd sayings . . ." Arianna said, reaching a door to the first basement level.

"I'm Canadian, actually . . ." Sam mutttered as he followed Arianna into a massive, bustling kitchen. It was abuzz with activity and steam and noise, with no less than fifty catering staff going about their jobs, oblivious to the security breach.

"You sure you know where you're going?" Sam asked as they wove their way through the kitchen.

"Yes," Arianna said. "Through this food hall, then we go down on the opposite side."

Sam followed her along a corridor and through thick wooden doors that led into a pantry the size of a decent supermarket.

"You know, now that I think about it, I think you're right about—"

"Shh!"

Arianna pulled him into a narrow space between tall stacks of boxed food as two cooks passed by carrying crates of expensive French champagne. They waited as they watched them disappear around a corner.

"Quick!" Arianna whispered, dragging Sam behind her and they ran to the far wall, around a corner and down to a different sub-basement. The vaulted brick ceiling seemed to stretch into gloomy infinity. Sam could see rows of dusty old wine bottles, lined up wall-to-wall alongside dimly glowing fridges full of shiny new bottles.

"Your country's leaders clearly like a drink," Sam said, inspecting a dusty bottle of Italian wine from 1968.

Arianna took out her phone and opened a map, studying

it to get her bearings. "I think we took a wrong turn," she said, the screen lighting up her face in the gloom.

"Yes . . ." a deep voice said from out of the dark shadows, startling them both. "You took a *very* wrong turn."

18

A heavy-set man emerged from the shadows with several uniformed security officers behind him.

"There's nowhere to run, Arianna," he said, his English pronunciation heavily altered by his thick accent.

It's not a Russian accent. But I know it . . .

"You cannot save your friend, he belongs to us. Don't you, *Sam?*"

That's when Sam recognized the voice, one that he'd heard before.

Hans.

It was the German billionaire treasure hunter, hell-bent on getting his hands on the ultimate prize beyond the Dream Gate.

The light bulb's glare glinted off his bald head, his sinister smile as menacing as ever.

"Arianna, I have not had the pleasure of meeting," Hans said. "You seem delightful—no matter which name you use. Did you *really* think it would take us long to work out who you were from the fake ID in Sam's dream?"

Arianna wisely remained quiet, glowering silently, glancing around at the guards.

"And then, our little Russian *feyyerverk*, I knew you would seek the help of your friend at the Kremlin," Hans went on. "You Dreamers, so predictable to the last."

"You're working with the Hypnos?" Sam asked Hans.

"Sure, why not?" Hans said. "What's important is that while we temporarily lost you there, we have captured you yet again inside of an hour."

"German efficiency, I suppose," Sam said.

Hans chuckled.

"You're kidding yourself, Hans," Sam said. He could see that the security guys were in fact German Guardians— the traitors who'd turned on Sam and his friends way back in Italy, now dressed as Kremlin guards. "It's sloppy work, letting one unarmed teenager get away from you. And it's not the first time I've outsmarted you."

"Hmm," Hans said. "Not sure if I'd put it that way. But let's just say that it will be the last."

"If you say so."

"I do." Hans looked behind to the wall of German Guardians. "We do. And once we've spent some time together in Siberia, I will know you, well, the inside of your mind, *very* well."

"Oh," Sam said, "you planned all this I suppose?"

Hans strode across the dark room to stand in front of Sam.

"You see," he said, "in the time that you have been here in Moscow, under our care and study, and your firecracker has been raiding our safe houses to try to find you, we've been, well, rather *busy*. Not only were you *kind* enough to bring me the last three Gears, but . . ."

He turned around and snapped his fingers, one of the German Guardians coming forward with a wooden box, which he handed to his boss. Hans opened the lid—

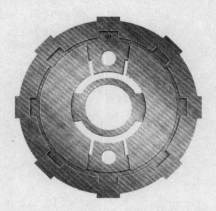

Sam was transfixed by the disc gleaming in the light—a Gear from the Bakhu machine, from the prophecy itself.

"You found the eighth Gear . . ." Sam said, looking up to see the glow from the Gear reflected onto Hans' round, greedy face. He glanced to Arianna, and could see the devastation in her eyes. "So Arianna was right?"

Hans' smile spoke of evil. He simply nodded.

Arianna looked to Sam—hot, vengeful tears trickling down her face.

"Arianna can't remember her dreams, but she's still been having them," Sam said. "And you've been watching, haven't you, Hans?"

She knows for sure now.

Sam turned away from the Gear, anger welling up inside him like a tidal wave.

19

EVA

"I'm so going to win a place on the team," Xavier said. "Even if I have to compete in a game to face my fears and steer dreams, I'm going to *demolish* these other guys. Demolish!"

"And girls?" Eva added.

"You know what I mean," Xavier said. "Guys is, like, guys. Like, you guys, that's all of you—guys and girls."

"If you say so," Eva said.

"Yeah," Xavier said. "And they are going to be devoured like . . . plankton . . . by a big . . . robot whale. That metaphor sort of unravelled as it went along, didn't it?"

"Kinda," Eva said. "I can see that a guy like you might struggle with that kind of thing."

"So how do we work this?" Gabriella asked, interrupting their banter.

"We dream, we see, we conquer," Xavier said. "Piece of cake."

"OK," Rapha replied. "Well, excuse my doubting mind, but you will be up against three groups of Dreamers who have been doing this for a lot longer than you have.

I believe you have about a sixty-six point six per cent chance, repeating, of course."

"That's not so bad," Eva said.

"Not of winning, of failing," Rapha said, clarifying his reckoning.

"Oh," Eva said. "But that still leaves a thirty-three per cent chance of success?"

"It's probably about zero. I was being kind," Rapha smiled apologetically.

"You think one of us will be in the final three to represent the school in the Doors?" Gabriella asked.

No one answered.

"We *are* part of the 13," Xavier said. "It'd make sense."

Maybe not all of us.

"There's far better Dreamers here than us," Maria said. "We may have dreamed of Gears, but steering dreams better than all the senior students who have been going to classes for years?"

"We'll be OK," Xavier said. "Got a third of a chance!" He grinned.

"Whose turn is it to host?" Gabriella asked.

"China," Xavier said, "representing the North-East quadrant. And reading the Dreamer news site, they've been preparing pretty hard."

"Good," Eva said. "Let them win this silly game."

There was a loud commotion inside the building. They all looked over from the lawn where they had been sprawled out under a large tree.

"I wonder what's going on?" Eva said.

Rapha ran inside and spoke to another student. When he came back he said, "It's those Dreamers—Cody and his parents—who Sam was with in Denver."

"They got out?" Eva said. "Then Sam might be out too!"

"Then . . . you don't know?" Eva said.

"No," Cody replied. "I'm sorry."

Eva was in the Professor's office. Cody and his parents were there, along with the Director, the Professor and Lora.

"And that's the last thing you saw?" Lora said. "The countdown ticking and Solaris with Sam?"

"Yes," Cody replied.

"Well, thank you for your honesty," the Professor replied, his tired face hopeful. "I've been told that you're now willing to assist us in the race?"

"We were foolish to believe Mac," Cody's father said. "And we'd like the opportunity to work with you now, to make it right."

Cody and his mother nodded in agreement.

"That is my understanding of the situation from our Agents who debriefed them," the Director said to the Professor.

"Then you are most welcome to join us here at the Academy."

All three of them looked relieved, tension ebbing out of the room.

"Thank you," Cody said.

"Eva, can you show our new student to the spare rooms in the western dorm?" the Professor asked.

She nodded, looking at Lora with some fire in her eyes. Lora gave an imperceptible look that Eva read as "*Cool it, now's not the time.*"

"Follow me," Eva said, leading Cody out of the room and through the grounds.

They walked in silence, but when they rounded the corner to the entrance, Eva waved to the others and they came over.

"Everyone," Eva said, "this is Cody, the Dreamer who brought Sam to Mac, and Solaris, in Denver. The last person to see our friend alive."

Cody turned to Eva, stunned, but Xavier was already coming in close and stood toe-to-toe with him. They were about the same size, though Eva thought that Cody looked stronger and more used to physical work.

But right now I'd put money on Xavier winning if it came to a fight.

"Sam is a *real* good friend of mine," Xavier said. "So tell us, moment-by-moment, *everything* that happened at the Grand Canyon and in Denver."

"And why you sold him out," Gabriella added.

Cody swallowed hard, then walked back out to the lawn and sat down. The others hesitated, then joined him.

"Alright, so first," Cody said, "Sam turned up at my tour office . . ."

SAM

Arianna *can still dream—she just can't remember her dreams.*

Sam felt exhilarated by the confirmation, and it gave him a sudden flash of clarity and purpose.

We need to escape, get the Gears from Hans and somehow restore Arianna's ability to dream. No sweat.

Sam weighed up the options before him and came to the swift conclusion: *not here.*

There were eight German Guardians present, dressed in the security outfit of the Kremlin Palace Guard that he'd seen outside in Red Square, pistols holstered by their sides.

Everything's changing. Or maybe there's a different set of rules for these guys—they're playing for keeps now.

But they won't kill me. Or Arianna. And if they don't have dart guns, they won't risk shooting us. So maybe we can outrun them, hide . . .

Maybe.

Sam stared at the two closest Guardians, one of whom looked somehow familiar.

The Guardian caught Sam's gaze and leaned toward

him. "Oh, you remember me? I remember you from our meeting outside Rome. You got lucky then. Good fortune is not on your side now," he spat out. He moved his hand to the gun at his side, chuckling with menace as Sam fought to control the urge to punch him in the face.

"You bang your head when you crashed in Italy?" Sam mocked. "Because you don't seem so smart these days."

The Guardian's face turned to thunder. He muttered under his breath as Sam took a step back and turned to look at Arianna. Her eyes were still locked on the Gear.

We have to leave it with Hans. Fight that battle another day.

Sam bumped Arianna and she looked across to him. Hans was still on the phone, talking in German. His tone was almost like a chastised child, as though he was being told off.

Maybe he's not such a big shot after all. Seems like everyone's got a boss somewhere.

"We have to get out of here," Sam whispered out of the corner of his mouth to her.

She nodded.

"I'll follow you," he said.

She looked at him like he was nuts.

"We can outrun them," Sam said. "Trust me, they won't shoot."

She looked from him to the Guardians, who stood before them, arms crossed, huge and intimidating, and

Sam could see that she came to the same realization as he had—that with the whole group in front of them, they'd made the tactical error of leaving them with an escape route.

Slowly they edged their way back a few steps.

Any head start is a good one.

The Guardian nearest to Arianna finally noticed them sidling away and reached out to grab hold of her. But it was too late. With the elegance and nimbleness of a ballerina, Arianna pivoted and broke into a flat-out run.

Sam was right behind her.

ALEX

"Tesla really did all that?" Alex said. They'd taken a break for lunch after clearing the room of dust and debris, and arranging the huge totems of Tesla's coils. Everything was prepped for the final power cable link up.

"Tesla was more than just one of our most important Dreamers," Shiva explained as they ate a few hot dogs from the street vendor outside the building. "They thought back then that he'd find the Dream Gate, and man, did he try! He managed to learn so much in one lifetime, he almost gained back what he thought we'd lost over a couple thousand years."

"Lost?"

"Yeah," Shiva said. "That was his belief, as well as that of many of the 19th century Dreamers. They thought that in ancient times, Dreamers had the ability to read each other's dreams and then lost it."

"A casualty of the Dark Ages?" Alex guessed.

"Exactly. Here, I'll show you a bit more . . ." Shiva said.

Shiva wiped the grime off his hands and used his tablet to patch into the Academy's secure site and read:

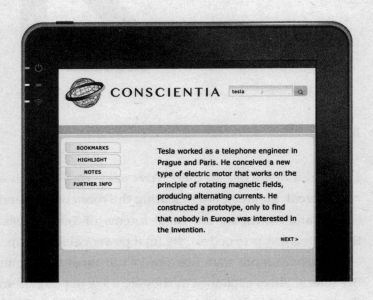

"Ah, electricity much, anyone?" Alex laughed.

"Yep. So, see here—it says he came to the US in 1884, where he worked for Thomas Edison, then established his own lab and obtained patents on his AC power system—including the coils, with initial support of the Dreamer Council."

"Nice."

"Then he came up against it. He was locked in a battle with Edison to convince the public of the efficiency and safety of alternating current over direct current and he succeeded in getting AC accepted as the electric power system worldwide."

"And he designed these coils to tap dreams?"

"A happy accident, as it turned out," Shiva said. "He was building the coils for wireless, free energy for the world when he stumbled across the Dreamscape."

"The electrical field that our dreams travel through, right?" Alex said.

"Yep. So he continued his dream work and returned to New York. With the encouragement and investment of a private backer, Tesla invented a new way of reading dreams via the dream waves in the atmosphere. In the end, he was moving too fast for everyone else—the Dreamer Council shut down his experiments pending further investigations. They wanted to be sure before rolling out his dream towers, before making them fully operational. Like the one at the Washington Monument and the Egyptian obelisk in Central Park."

"There's an Egyptian obelisk in Central Park? Here, in New York?"

Shiva nodded. "Sure, Cleopatra's needle."

"Huh, of course. But I just don't get why they'd shut Tesla down."

"He proposed something that was too advanced for the Council, especially at that time."

"What was that?"

"He figured out a way to *transmit* dreams, not just receive them."

"What does that mean?" Alex asked.

"It means," Shiva said, "that Tesla figured out a way to

transplant dreams into *other* people. He could send energy into the wave and make whole cities have dreams—or nightmares. The Council was worried that in the wrong hands, that kind of technology could become a weapon."

"And that's why he was shunned from the Dreamer world."

"Yep. He died an old, poor man, never seeing the true potential of his greatest invention. Pretty harsh stuff," Shiva sighed.

"And what was he using as the antenna for these coils?" Alex asked. "Towers like the obelisk in Central Park?"

"Yes, at first, but then he found that he needed to use the tallest structure around," Shiva smiled.

"Tallest? Like a skyscraper?"

"Yep. These coils here were hardwired into what was the tallest building in the world at that time."

"What, is it gone now?"

"No. It's still standing, it's just taller ones have been built now." Shiva ate the last of his hot dog and tossed the wrapper across the room into a trash can in a three-pointer. "In fact, it's in this very city . . . it's the Empire State Building."

"Try again!" Alex called out from Tesla's lab.

Shiva threw the switch.

Alex stood up and watched the towering coil.

Nothing happened.

"You sure you connected it?" Shiva called down.

"Sure. You sure you flicked the right switch?"

"Yes!"

"Try again," Alex said, wiping his grimy hands on a rag.

FLICK.

Nothing.

"And you definitely reversed the polarity?" Shiva called.

Alex looked up and saw his friend's head and shoulders looking down through the trapdoor that led to the big, old vaulted lab above. He pulled a face at him and Shiva laughed. Alex wiped off the sweat trickling into his eyes. It was hot and humid, and he was covered in black grease and grime.

"Maybe Tesla wasn't such a genius after all," Alex said. "Or maybe we need to fuel up the flux capacitor."

"Ha, ha."

"Check everything and we'll try one more time," Shiva said. "Then we'll call it impossible and move onto the next option—a full rewire."

"Nothing's impossible," Alex said under his breath as he crouched back down, then stopped himself from disconnecting the thick power cables.

Nothing's impossible? Where'd that saying come from?

He closed his eyes a minute. It was a phrase seared into his psyche, a distant long-term memory stored away for some specific reason.

My mother? Did she ever say that? Maybe.

No.

Then who? My father?

No. Couldn't be. I couldn't remember anything about him.

Could I?

"Alex?"

He looked up and saw Shiva looking down at him again.

"Are you OK down there? Or have you succumbed to your own putrid fumes?"

"What putrid fumes?"

"Don't think that I can't smell what that breakfast burrito and four hot dogs have done to your digestive system."

"Ha, right," Alex said, snapping out of his reverie and double-checking the power cables and the polarity—

Which he hadn't reversed.

Oops.

Alex switched the cables around. "Try again!" he called out.

"Stand back," Shiva said for the hundredth time, the warning near redundant as nothing had happened yet.

This time there was a low but distinct whooping sound. It went on for about five seconds.

"Did you hear that?" Alex shouted, jumping in excitement. Shiva looked down at him, incredulous. "It switched on!"

"I know!"

"It sounded like the Millennium Falcon, trying to get to hyperspace—but failing!"

"I know!"

"Why'd it not stay on?"

"We tripped the circuit breakers. We need more power."

"Where are we going to get that from?" Alex asked.

Shiva looked blank and then his white teeth flashed in a blinding smile. "I think I know just the place!"

SAM

Sam could hear the commotion among the Guardians as they reacted.

Back at the pantry, they raced through the corridors between stacks of boxed food, racks of wine and seemingly endless shelves stocked with all kinds of jars.

Sam could hear footfalls on the stone floor. It sounded like a herd of buffaloes was stampeding behind them.

And closing in.

Sam glanced behind, just in time to see—

WHACK!

Sam reached out and pulled Arianna around a corner just as a net was fired by one of the German Guardians. The wire mesh and weighted perimeter slammed into a barrel of borscht, the wood shattering and the purple-coloured pickled cabbage erupting like a volcano.

Sam saw most of the Guardians slip over and get tangled in a huge pile-up among the mess.

One Guardian was at the back, bringing the net-launcher down from his shoulder and grimacing as he saw his friends slip and slide their way on the floor.

One final Guardian was still in hot pursuit.

They burst through the doors to the kitchen. Hot steam and noise surrounded them—a sea of cooks prepping the day's food service.

Sam and Arianna ran side-by-side through the aisles between kitchen benches, behind a battalion of pastry chefs, under a massive tray of dumplings, around a—

Sam lost his footing, slipping on a wet patch of the tiled floor, and landed heavily on his back. He slid forward.

Arianna turned, a huge wooden rolling pin in her hands, and Sam watched as if in slow motion as it swiped only millimetres clear over his head.

WHOOMP!

The sound it made as it connected with the Guardian's stomach was like all the air being beaten out of a mattress.

"Nice shot!" Sam said. Arianna helped him to his feet and they ran on without looking back. "What's next?"

"Next?" she asked.

"Where are we going now?"

"To plan B," Arianna said.

"What's plan B?" Sam asked as they entered a large hall and resumed a more normal pace to save being noticed by the palace's real security guards.

"We get out of town the old fashioned way."

The old-fashioned way turned out to be train. A big train, an *old* train. In a very beautiful station, like you'd see in a classic movie.

"I like trains," Sam said to Arianna, who was next to him, tickets in her hand, as they headed for a carriage near the end of the platform. "You know where they're going."

"Yes, to Siberia," she replied.

"No, I mean I like them because you know where they're going."

"Yes," she said, looking at him weirdly.

"No, I mean, you know, because of the tracks . . ."

"Yes?"

"Ah, forget it."

Arianna laughed. Sam liked how her face lit up when she laughed.

She hasn't had much to laugh about for a while.

"What's so funny?" he replied.

"I know what you mean, Sam," Arianna replied. "You like to travel on trains because they are predictable, they have a schedule and tracks, and you can rely on where they will be taking you."

"Yeah, maybe I could have said it that way," Sam said, stepping aside to allow her to enter the carriage, the last of the first-class sleepers. "And to think, English is your second language."

"My third actually, after Russian and German," Arianna

said. "That reminds me, if we get caught, or questioned by anybody, don't speak. I'll do all the talking."

"Just like last time," Sam said. "Got it."

"Relax," Arianna said, opening the door to their cabin, "you look suspicious when you look that nervous."

"But I *am* nervous," Sam replied out of the corner of his mouth. A group of railway workers entered the carriage and the two of them went into their cabin and closed the door.

"You'll attract attention looking like that," she persisted.

"I can't help it," Sam said. "I'm waiting for my positive train vibe to kick in."

A couple of police officers walked past on the platform outside. Serious-looking guys on patrol, submachine guns slung over their shoulders. Arianna pulled down the blind.

Sam tested out the beds—one was in the sofa, the other pulled down from behind the wall panel. Other than that, there was a little table, and a tiny bathroom with a toilet and washbasin.

"How long is this trip?" he asked.

"With all the stops, about twenty hours," she said, reading from a brochure.

"That long?"

"It's good—it will give Boris time to prepare for our arrival."

"Prepare?"

"The Nyx. This is it for us—we're going to strike the

Hypnos where it hurts, their science facility." Arianna peered out through a gap between the window and the blind.

"The coast clear?"

"The coast is a long way away."

"I mean . . . man, I really gotta start talking properly."

"Gotta?"

"Don't worry about it. So, what you got in that bag?"

"A phone, but it's not completely secure," Arianna said, rummaging through her bag and pulling out its contents. "Plus, let us see . . . bottle of water, wallet, passport, taser—"

"You *are* prepared," Sam said. "So when can I make a call?"

"Our first major stop," she said, checking the train timetable for information. "In six hours, we stop for fifteen minutes to take on fuel and uncouple the last few carriages. We can take a small risk to use a public phone so you can contact your friends."

Sam nodded.

"You sure you want to do this?" Sam said.

"This? You mean getting my ability to dream back?"

"Yes."

"*Da*, of course. Since I was ten, when they took it from me, I have had, how would you say this, day terrors?"

"Like nightmares in waking life?"

"Yes. Images, moments, times when I am scared. I see things that are not there but are in my mind."

"Well, just don't taser me when I'm looking the other

way," Sam said, and it lightened the mood. "What do you know about this place we're going to?"

"If you thought the Kremlin was imposing as a fortress, you will be surprised."

"Is this place so massively fortified because they want to keep people like us out?" Sam asked.

"And because it's a prison. A long time ago it was a labour camp where they sent political enemies. Now it is deserted but for a small facility for the Dreamers."

"Hmm, another place to break into . . ."

"Sam," Arianna said, looking at him with a steady gaze and holding his shoulders. "You want this, correct? You need this Gear."

He nodded. "I need to get all the Gears back and it sounds like that's where Hans is going. So . . ."

"You survived flying around the world in a supersonic escape pod," Arianna said. "This will be a, how would you say, a walk through the park?"

"A walk in the park," Sam said.

"OK," Arianna smiled warmly, a big genuine grin that spread through her face to her eyes. "A walk in the park. So, we can do this?"

"Break *into* a prison? Sure, why not?" Sam smiled.

"Then let us do this."

"Let's do this," Sam corrected.

"Huh?"

"Nothing," Sam said. "It'll be a walk in the park . . ."

EVA

"**S**o," Xavier said, after Cody had told them all his story and fielded dozens of questions, "you tricked Sam into going down into the Grand Canyon with you, even though you'd already found the Gear and given it to your parents. Then you let him be taken to this mysterious underground government bunker, and left him as you ran away via an escape pod."

"Yes," Cody replied. He looked directly at Xavier, forcing himself to hold his gaze, even as his cheeks reddened.

At least he's not trying to hide the facts.

"And you left our friend behind," Gabriella added.

"I couldn't—" Cody began.

"You're a coward," Xavier said, walking off.

Eva looked at the faces of her friends all gathered around. They looked a little stunned, as though the information they'd just learned neither settled anything nor gave them much reason for hope.

"We didn't know that Mac was crazy and had gone out on his own, I promise you all that," Cody said. "We thought we were doing the best thing, the *right* thing."

"We get it," Eva said after a moment's silence among the group. "We have to put it behind us. We're never going to make it if we don't pull together."

The others nodded, Maria reaching out to tap Cody's arm.

Cody nodded and appeared relieved and thankful. "What about Xavier?" he asked.

"He's a little hot in the head," Gabriella said, and the others laughed. "What?"

"Hotheaded," Eva said. "Yes, he is. Plus, he's known Sam the longest, they knew each other back at school."

"Oh," Cody said. "Fair enough."

"What was he like?" Rapha asked Cody. "This Solaris guy? Nobody's really seen him up close, or for very long."

"He's tall," Cody said. "Dressed all in black. Full face mask. And his voice . . . terrifying. All scrambled and metallic, amplified. Sounded like it was a respirator—like he needs it to breathe. Just like in our nightmares, really. But scarier."

Eva could tell that it was haunting Cody.

Good, let him be a bit haunted . . . maybe that'll help him remember what we're fighting against.

"I've been thinking about it—him—a lot this past week. I see him, I hear him, in every dream I've had since. They all end the same—he shoots me with fire."

The group was silent.

"Come on, guys," Eva said, getting to her feet. "Time to call it a day."

They all made their separate ways to their dorms.

"Follow me," Eva said to Cody, showing him the way.

"You said you've been there before?" he asked.

"Where?" Eva said as they headed up the stairs.

"The Grand Canyon," he replied.

"My dad took me on a tour when I was a little girl," she said. "Had you ever been to that Bureau 13 site in Denver before?"

They stopped outside a door that Eva opened, revealing an empty room for Cody.

"No, I hadn't," Cody said. "But my parents had spoken about it. They explained that if there was ever a crisis that we would head there, that there was a facility for a special group of the government elite, and that we'd be able to join them and be taken to safety."

"How?"

"There are deep bunkers there, under the mountains. And subway lines linking them all. A full underground city, able to house half a million people. Top secret, of course, and just for senior government and their families, essential people and all that. It was made to withstand an all-out nuclear war."

Eva looked at him. "Do you think Sam got out?"

Cody didn't hesitate. "Yes," he said. "I have no doubt. I was shouting to him, telling him I'd wait, but he told me to go, that he was right behind me. And—and there was something about Solaris, almost like he cared about what happened to Sam. He would have got out with him, or maybe they made their escape separately. But they definitely got out."

Eva felt her eyes water at the thought of Sam being stuck somewhere with Solaris.

Please don't let that be the case.

"And these pods, do you know where they went?"

"No. Apparently they can travel to anywhere in the world."

"Where did you land?"

"San Antonio."

"Why there?"

"That's where we landed because by the time my dad figured out how to override the controls and force a touch-down, we were flying over the place."

"So Sam could be anywhere," Eva said. "Anywhere in the world."

"Yep. I'm so sorry, I had no idea what was going on. I feel so stupid now."

Eva walked away down the hall, then turned. "You'll get your chance to make up for it, you know," she said. "One day, you'll have a chance to prove to all of us that you can be trusted, that you *are* worthy of being one of the last 13."

Cody nodded.

"Until then," Eva said as she walked away, "and until Sam is found safe, it's probably best to keep a low profile around here."

"I will," Cody said. "And Eva?"

She turned back to face him once more.

"Thanks," he said.

Eva nodded and left, a spring in her step as she rushed to see Jedi about locating Sam's escape pod.

24

SAM

S am looked out the window of their train carriage. The train was huge—two massive diesel locomotives up front and another at the end of the ten passenger cars and a dozen or so freight cars. "This is Siberia?"

"Yes. It is a big place, vast, mostly empty of people, though that is changing," Arianna said. "To understand the size, think of it like this—Siberia is bigger than the whole of America. Canada too. You're from there, correct?"

"I was raised my whole life in Canada, apart from a couple years in the States."

"Why'd you go there?"

"My parents' work."

"Why'd you move back to Canada?"

Sam looked absently out the window, watching the endless trees and open plains and mountains, the occasional farmhouse and road flitting past. He didn't register much of it, instead thinking of his friend, Bill, and the fire that had taken his life . . .

"It's complicated," Sam said. "There was an accident. My

parents thought we should move back to where I had old friends. And my psychologist was there."

"Accident?" she asked.

Sam nodded. There was silence between them for a while, then he asked, "So where are we getting off the train?"

"Krasnoyarsk, hundreds of kilometres from here. Then we'll borrow a friend's car and drive from there."

"To where I dreamed about the cabin?"

"Yes."

"With the wolves."

"Right . . ."

They watched the scene framed by the window in silence.

"You've been away from your home for a while?" Sam said.

"My home is a suitcase. I live a gypsy life, on the road, where my work takes me."

"Work? You're, what, sixteen?"

"Yes. I study, by computer, but I compete in gymnastics. The training is constant."

"Did you go to school for that?"

"Until I was thirteen, and since then it has been remote schooling, on the road with my parents and online with my school teachers. Then I can also go to competitions around the world."

"Do you like it?" Sam asked.

"Gymnastics?"

"Yeah."

"Yes. It was what I used to dream of doing," Arianna said. "My last dream that I can remember was competing in the Olympics some day. I still hold that dream."

"That's pretty amazing. How about regular school, do you miss that?"

"Yes, and no," Arianna said, a slight smile on her face. "Mostly I miss old school friends, but I still see them sometimes, and I've made plenty of new ones through competitions and practice. What about you—do you miss your school?"

Sam nodded. "In a way, though I haven't really had time to miss it too much."

"Time . . ." Arianna said. "Not enough time . . . that's what so many people say these days, as an excuse, *da*?"

"Yeah," Sam said, "I guess. Though with this race to get the Gears, to beat everyone else to the Dream Gate, we really *are* in a race against time."

Arianna nodded and they sat for a while, absently watching the view rolling by outside the window as the train headed east across the vast landscape.

"What's your hometown like?" Arianna asked, taking a sip from her water bottle and passing it to Sam.

"Vancouver?" Sam said, taking a drink while he thought about it. "It's quiet, nice—friendly. It's the place I've spent the most time in, so it's familiar and comfortable."

"All this time trying to save the world—you are travelling like me. So I ask, you miss it?"

"Yeah, totally," Sam said. "I miss a few friends, my dog, my school, my hockey buddies, my jujitsu classes. And the city, I miss that too. The mornings can be so perfect you could lose a whole day to them."

"Lose a day to the morning?" Arianna quizzed.

"Figure of speech."

"Right. And your family? You miss them?"

"Yeah, I miss them too," Sam said. "I guess I just miss life as a regular teenager, laughing with friends, an easier time . . . before all this craziness."

"Before you had the, what is it called, the *fate*? Yes, the fate of the entire world in your hands."

"Yep, that's about the size of it," Sam said, and with not much else to say in response to that, they laughed.

EVA

Eva lay in the dark, happy to be awake and not to be dreaming. The light of the moon shone brightly through the open curtains.

At least I'm not having a nightmare.

Not another nightmare about Sam, as she'd had so many times since he'd been missing.

"Can you sleep?" Gabriella asked.

"No, not really," Eva replied.

"He'll be alright," Gabriella said. "I know it, now that we have heard from Cody. Before that, I was worried."

"You never seemed worried," Eva scoffed.

"Well, I *was*," Gabriella said. "You have to feel a bit better about it now, right?"

"Maybe."

"Not maybe. Solaris would not harm him—"

"Yes, he would."

"Well, he wouldn't kill him."

Eva was silent for a while.

"You're right," Eva said. "He can't kill him. He needs him just as we do."

They were silent then, and Eva listened as her roommate started to quietly snore, and eventually she too slept.

A restless sleep.

The next morning, Eva entered the Professor's study. Lora and Jedi were waiting there with him.

"Take a seat," the Professor said.

Eva sat next to Lora. "Before we begin, can I ask something?"

"Of course," the Professor said, Lora nodding in agreement. "What is it, Eva?"

"It's about Cody, and his parents . . . I know they were tricked by Mac and it seems like they're with us now. But—but how . . ."

"How can we be sure they're *really* with us?" Lora added. "Is that what you're asking?"

"Well, yes. Ever since this race started, everyone has been switching sides faster than I can keep up with. We've been betrayed by the Egyptian and German Guardians, the Enterprise split in two when Stella went rogue . . ."

"You're quite right to be concerned, Eva," the Professor said. "We agree that we must be cautious. Cody and his parents have been welcomed here but they are all being very closely watched and their access to certain things and certain information is currently restricted. We will

EVA

Eva lay in the dark, happy to be awake and not to be dreaming. The light of the moon shone brightly through the open curtains.

At least I'm not having a nightmare.

Not another nightmare about Sam, as she'd had so many times since he'd been missing.

"Can you sleep?" Gabriella asked.

"No, not really," Eva replied.

"He'll be alright," Gabriella said. "I know it, now that we have heard from Cody. Before that, I was worried."

"You never seemed worried," Eva scoffed.

"Well, I *was*," Gabriella said. "You have to feel a bit better about it now, right?"

"Maybe."

"Not maybe. Solaris would not harm him—"

"Yes, he would."

"Well, he wouldn't kill him."

Eva was silent for a while.

"You're right," Eva said. "He can't kill him. He needs him just as we do."

They were silent then, and Eva listened as her roommate started to quietly snore, and eventually she too slept.

A restless sleep.

The next morning, Eva entered the Professor's study. Lora and Jedi were waiting there with him.

"Take a seat," the Professor said.

Eva sat next to Lora. "Before we begin, can I ask something?"

"Of course," the Professor said, Lora nodding in agreement. "What is it, Eva?"

"It's about Cody, and his parents . . . I know they were tricked by Mac and it seems like they're with us now. But—but how . . ."

"How can we be sure they're *really* with us?" Lora added. "Is that what you're asking?"

"Well, yes. Ever since this race started, everyone has been switching sides faster than I can keep up with. We've been betrayed by the Egyptian and German Guardians, the Enterprise split in two when Stella went rogue . . ."

"You're quite right to be concerned, Eva," the Professor said. "We agree that we must be cautious. Cody and his parents have been welcomed here but they are all being very closely watched and their access to certain things and certain information is currently restricted. We will be very careful until we can be sure that we completely trust them."

Eva sighed. "That's good to know, thank you."

"So, with that matter dealt with," the Professor said, leaning forward on his elbows, "I believe you had quite the dream last night. We've just watched the replay and it's quite intriguing. One particular image especially."

"Intriguing?" Eva said.

"This," Jedi said, bringing up an image, "is the Dendera Zodiac. In 1799, a French artist called Denon found, and drew, a copy of the circular zodiac, which was discovered in a temple ceiling in Dendera in Egypt."

"How does this help us?" Eva asked.

"You'll see," the Professor said.

"In 1820," Jedi went on, flicking through digital images, "the ceiling was taken apart and transported to France. It ended up in the Louvre, where it's still on display today. Experts examined it and calculated that it dates back to 50 BCE, going on the placement of the five planets in the design, a pattern that occurs only once every thousand years."

"OK," Eva said. "I remember dreaming about something like this, but I was definitely not in the Louvre in my dream. And what I saw was a bit different to that."

"Exactly!" Jedi said. "The Dendera Zodiac is a map of the stars, showing the twelve constellations of the zodiac. These were used in the ancient Egyptian calendar, which was based on lunar cycles of about thirty days, and so on."

Pictures of the zodiac as Eva knew it flickered up on the screen.

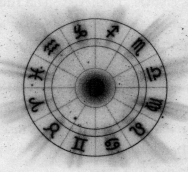

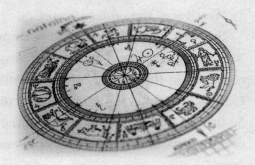

"And this is vital news to us because . . ." Eva's eyes were starting to glass over.

"Because," Lora said, jumping in, "as you said, what you dreamed about last night was *not* the Dendera Zodiac."

Jedi changed pictures. Now the screen showed another kind of zodiac.

"*This* is much older, about a thousand years or so," the Professor said, "say around 1300–1200 BCE."

"During the reign of Ramses the Great," Lora clarified, to stress the relevance.

"Notice anything significant about it?" Jedi said.

Eva stood and studied it closely, not sure at first, then stepped back to see it better.

This one has twelve signs. But what's that in the middle? A thirteenth sign?

SAM

"**W**hat about you?" Sam asked. "What's your story?"

"My story probably sounds like a sad one, but it has a happy ending," Arianna said.

Sam was silent and let her continue in her own time.

Her steely eyes flickered vacantly at the landscape rushing by out the window.

"The sad part is right at the start," she said, "I never knew my real parents. I was in an orphanage. I was told later that they had been killed—an accident, on the road."

"Oh, man. I'm sorry."

"It's been a long time. I was just a baby, so it's all I've ever really known."

Sam was silent.

"It's OK . . . I was in state care and got lucky, very lucky—so many are not—I was almost immediately adopted."

"This is in Moscow?" Sam asked.

"St. Petersburg," she said, twitching at the sound of the train blasting its horn as it shot through a crossing. "At least at first. I grew up there, then we were in Moscow for some time, then a few years in Germany, where I went to an international school and received special gymnastics training."

"Sounds like your adoptive parents were very supportive," Sam said.

Arianna nodded.

"They are the best kind of people. Then, when I was about twelve, some government agents from Moscow turned up, along with the local German authorities, and explained that the paperwork had been incorrect, that my parents hadn't been killed after all."

"*What?*"

"It was a lie. Of course we didn't know it then. It's what the Hypnos do—take Dreamers from their families and put them into orphanages so that they can be brainwashed. But a mistake was made—I was never meant to be adopted. They showed up, and they took me to this place in Siberia. There was nothing my parents could do. I was taken to the science facility we are going to now. That's where they put the chip in my head to steal the dreams."

"But you got out," Sam said.

"I made a good show of pretending that I accepted their methods, played the part of being the good girl. So after a couple of months, once they knew the chip was working, they let me leave. I went straight to our family friends in Krasnoyarsk, where we're headed now."

"Have the Hypnos ever tried to find you?"

"Maybe, I don't know. My parents and I changed our

names, I dyed my hair and changed my appearance in the last four years, and we never spend too long in the same area. That's why you saw the wrong name in your dream. Nika Garin is the name I'm using at the moment, but my real name is Arianna—Arianna Barinova." She smiled shyly.

"Wow, so you've really had a life on the run, in a way?" Sam asked.

She nodded. "I don't think the chips can track locations, at least not the one I was given back then, so I wanted to disappear, get the Hypnos out of my life as much as possible."

"I can totally understand that, I would too. But it's great you were able to be with your parents again, and that they appreciate gymnastics."

Arianna smiled. "They're Russian, gymnastics is in our blood, ha! But yes, they're great—they support any dream that I want to follow . . . dream . . . that's funny . . ." she trailed off.

"Let's try and get some rest," Sam said. "What's ahead is going to be intense."

"Intense?" Arianna asked.

"Crazy."

"Ah. And so far this day has not been crazy enough for you?"

Sam smiled. "So far it's like any other Wednesday for me. But yeah, I'm thinking it's going to get much more crazy."

"Good," Arianna said. "I like a little crazy, especially when it comes to finally taking on the Hypnos."

Neither Sam nor Arianna could sleep, so they bought food from the diner car and played with an old deck of cards for dried fruit and nuts. The refuelling stop had been and gone. Sam tried to use a pay phone to call the Academy but, frustratingly, it was out of service. Sam's attempts to borrow a phone to make an international call were greeted with stony silences and a distinct lack of offered phones.

I guess I'll just have to be "missing" for a few hours longer.

Sam tried not to think about how worried everyone at the Academy would be.

I am supposed to be saving the world, after all. What would they do if I did end up being . . . gone? Who's the back-up Sam?

"Can you tell me more about your time at this place?" Sam asked, flaking out at cards again and cursing his lack of concentration.

It took Arianna a while to answer. "It's where they take us," she said. "All the known Dreamers."

"What? In the whole of Russia?"

"Yes."

"How long were you there for?"

"Months."

"What happened?"

"They conducted tests. They set it up like a school, but we realized that we were all there for our dreams. They tried controlling how much we slept and used different kinds of drugs to see what effects they had. When I saw that those who were obedient but of no use were let go, I made sure that I flunked out as soon as possible."

"And the Dreamer chip thing?"

She turned around in her seat, holding her ponytail of red hair out of the way. Near the top of her spine at the back of her head, was a tiny white vertical scar.

"That's *it*?" Sam said.

"Yes," she replied, sitting back. "I've heard stories that the Nyx used to try to remove them, but it never worked out. It's practically inside the spinal column."

"Wow, that's horrible," Sam said.

"Thank you."

"I don't mean that *you're* horrible!"

She smiled. "Yes, I know."

"And you guys have never tried to take on this facility in Siberia before?"

"No." Arianna looked out at the landscape, which was now a grey-white scene of barren farmland and distant wilderness. "Apart from the natural defences, as a former high-security military site it is still guarded around the clock."

"And why do you think you can storm the compound now?"

Arianna gave a sly grin. "Because we have discovered another way in," she replied. "And it's how we're going to shut it down once and for all."

27

The town had a name, though Sam couldn't pronounce it. It was more a collection of roadhouses and mechanics' workshops along what was wide enough to be a four-lane highway but lacked any painted lane markings. They crunched their way across the snow to the meeting place—a truck-stop diner that, aside from the prices and signage, would have looked just as at home in North America.

Boris had traded his beaten-up taxi for a four-wheel drive that looked three times older than Sam. He was waiting inside, behind the frosted glass, giving a thumbs up and breaking into a grin at their appearance from the train.

"What I would give to have my Stealth Suit back," Sam said, rubbing his hands together as they walked.

"Your what?" Arianna looked puzzled.

"Stealth Suit," Sam said. "It's made from a type of material that changes to whatever the wearer wants or needs. Right now, I'd have mine be a wrap-around feather quilt . . . man, I think I'd sleep standing up if that were the case. Is it always this cold here?"

"No," Arianna said. "It should not be like this. The weather has gone upside down."

"Upside-down weather for an upside-down world," Sam muttered to himself. He opened the door for Arianna, and immediately the heat from inside the diner blew out and greeted them, along with the smells of breakfast which made Sam's stomach grumble.

They exchanged greetings and gave Boris an explanation of what had occurred at the Kremlin.

"Can I use your phone to call my friends?" Sam asked Boris finally.

"It's dead out here," Boris replied. "Only satellite phones work long distance here."

"There may be a pay phone," Arianna said, looking around.

"I'll check," Sam said, and went for a walk. He found the pay phone by the bathrooms, picked up the receiver and put it to his ear.

Then he realized that the cord was cut.

He replaced the receiver.

The phone was broken, probably years ago, and had since turned into a planter box for mould and some bright yellow toadstools.

"Great, do no phones work in Russia?" he said and ambled back to the table. The diner was full of steam and the smell of bacon and onions cooking. "No luck again."

"Someone on the team will have a satellite phone at the farmhouse," Boris said.

"The team?"

"For our Hypnos assault," he replied. "They're meeting us there in about twelve hours."

"How many people are in the team?" Sam asked.

"About fifty. All ready to take over the facility."

The waitress came over and asked for their order. Either her tone or local dialect confused Sam's earpiece, so without a translation, Sam simply looked at the menu and pointed, and five minutes later he had a cup of coffee, a glass of apple juice, and three plates of food.

"Oh, these are good," Sam said, heaving down his second plate of dumplings. "What do you call these?"

"Pierogi."

"What's the meat in them?" Sam said, adding hot sauce from a basket of condiments on the table. "Lamb? Beef? Man, they're delicious."

Arianna conferred with Boris, and they laughed and she said to Sam, "Boris calls such meat fillings in establishments like this . . . how do you say this—mystery meat?"

Sam swallowed hard.

A memory returned, swirled around the back of his mind.

A diner. Not unlike this one.

Sam smiled.

Tobias and I were in a diner like this, before Denver.

"What is it?" Arianna said, eating a roll of cheese and bright purple borscht.

"A memory, of a friend from back home," Sam said slowly.

"Where's your friend now?" Boris asked.

Sam's smile faded. "I'm not sure . . . we got separated. He was in Texas when I was in Denver."

"Ah, yes." Arianna said. Again she spoke rapid-fire Russian with Boris, who then got out his backpack and passed a file over the table. "This is what we could find on Denver."

Sam opened the file—it was a stack of printouts from news websites.

The first headline read:

Nuclear Disaster Narrowly Averted

at Denver International Airport

The article that followed explained the incident as a radiation leak from a plane at the airport. But other articles were quick to poke holes in the official story, suggesting a cover-up of everything from a military training exercise gone wrong to pointing the finger at foreign extremists or a possible explosion at a nearby nuclear processing facility.

"I can't believe that I was there . . ." Sam said.

"Your escape pod was jettisoned from a facility there called the Ark," Arianna said.

"I don't remember an escape pod. I don't remember how I got out . . . or what happened." Sam closed the file, not wanting to think about the fate of the others he'd known to be there, let alone all the civilians who may have been caught up in the mayhem.

"You will remember," Arianna said. "This time tomorrow, your memory will double. In a week, it will be yours again—back to normal, I mean."

"Great, then I'll just forget the little things."

"Little things?"

"Yeah," Sam said, "like forgetting to brush my teeth and feed the dog, stuff like that."

"You brush your dog's teeth?" Boris said.

They laughed.

"Actually, I think my mom *did* brush Scout's teeth," Sam said, then he went quiet as he recalled his family.

Where are they?

His strained memories were interrupted when Boris brought out another file from his bag, this one with several maps and schematics.

"This is from the explosion that happened at Tunguska in 1908," Arianna explained. "Reported to the public as an asteroid collision, but it is crucial to us in other ways."

"Why?" Sam asked, flicking through the notes.

"We believe the site was the location of Russia's first attempt at building a Tesla-type dreaming tower."

"And that is . . ."

"That is how they used to read dreams," Arianna said. "By tapping into a little-known frequency that transmits through the earth's ionosphere."

"Right, right, of course, the Tesla frequency," Sam added. "Like the antenna used at the Eiffel Tower by the Dreamer Council," Sam said.

"Yes," she replied. "You know about that?"

"Know it?" Sam said. "I was at the Tower when the Council was attacked by that traitor Mac and his cronies. I went from the secret chambers underneath it all the way to the top, and off it, that day!"

"You will have to tell me about it sometime," Arianna said.

"I will," Sam replied. "But tell me about Tunguska."

"We don't know exactly what happened, but somehow the explosion there wiped the facility off the map. The new one was built underground and they have devised a way to direct an electronic beam into the atmosphere, doing away with antennas."

"And they're reading people's dreams that way?"

"Reading, stealing, take your pick."

"And that's where they take Dreamers to implant them with these microchips."

"Yes."

"So," Sam said. "How exactly are we going to break into this place?"

Boris broke into a huge grin.

ALEX

"City Hall?" Alex said, looking up at the imposing building in downtown Manhattan, across the road from their subterranean hide-out where they'd been tinkering with the monolithic Tesla coils. "You're going to steal power from City Hall?"

"It's got masses of power going in," Shiva said. "And sky-high generating capacity."

"And how do you propose we get in," Alex asked, noting the cops milling about, "let alone tap into their power grid and siphon off a few megawatts?"

"Well, we are from the power company, after all," Shiva said, changing their Stealth Suits to appear as government electricians. "And we're not going in the front door. We're going under."

Alex shook his head. "I just knew you were going to say that. But man, if we get caught—I've been in trouble with the law here before, they don't fool around."

"Then we don't get caught."

"They'll think we're terrorists," Alex persisted.

"Relax," Shiva said. "We're not going to get caught."

"I think that'll do us," Shiva said, triple-checking the connection. "Yep, I'm sure of it. Come on, let's go."

Alex followed Shiva, making their way through the electrical access tunnel that snaked under the road.

"How do you know that it'll be enough power for what we need to do?" Alex asked, as Shiva gave him a hand out of the narrow tunnel full of dust and grime.

"It's heaps," Shiva said. "Just you wait and see."

They stood in the exchange room where several tunnels split off.

"This one," Alex said, leading the way. Up ahead they could see a glow stick that Alex had left behind.

"You're a regular Hansel and Gretel," Shiva said.

At the end of the tunnel Alex pushed through the hatch and helped his friend through.

"You look like you've been working in the coal mines," Shiva said.

"You know, when I was a kid and had daydreams of working 'undercover,' it was more in a secret spy, James Bond type of way," Alex said. "I never figured I'd be literally sneaking around under a city."

"That's why one must be careful, and precise, in what one wishes for, my friend," Shiva chuckled.

"Yeah, well, you don't look so shiny yourself," Alex teased back. "So what were you gonna be when you grew up?"

"Me? Well, apart from being an international singing sensation, I'm actually living the dream," Shiva smiled.

"You know, Gabriella's one of the last 13, you should ask her for advice," Alex said. "But in the meantime, don't give up your day job!"

"A good tip, my friend, but for now, let me see about this hookup," Shiva said as they arrived back at the main control panel. He flicked the switch—

Sparks flew and Shiva was blown backwards across the room.

"Whoa!" Alex said, helping Shiva to his feet. "You OK?"

Shiva nodded. The soles of his shoes were smoking—the rubber melted to a gooey toffee.

Alex blinked away the smoke. "I think we're going to need a bigger fuse box."

SAM

The Nyx assault team were waiting for them when they arrived. They were a mixed group of varying ages, all dressed in mismatched winter clothes. None of them appeared to be carrying weapons.

They assembled in a huge barn on the edge of a forest some fifty kilometres from their objective—the Hypnos site in Tunguska.

"OK, listen up!" Boris said in Russian. He stood on a workbench, addressing the assembled crowd around him, most with cups of steaming hot tea or coffee huddled in their hands. "I will explain the teams that you are in, and then you will go to your team leaders for more briefing. Make no mistake—we go tonight—and we take them out once and for all!"

A cheer spread through the crowd, many raising their cups in jubilation. Sam looked into their faces and saw that they were ecstatic at the prospect ahead.

Don't they realize how dangerous this plan is?

"So," Boris went on, shining a laser light against a large map of the area taped to the wall behind him, "we will be getting backup from our friends here in the local community and those soldiers who are loyal to our cause. The roads will be cut off by earthmoving equipment, so the Hypnos will have no way in or out. The power will be out, but they have emergency generators for the lights. All radio waves will be jammed by our friend Grigory—"

A young guy at the back of the group raised his hand and several people nearby clapped him on the back.

"And on the launch of the flare, we all move in," Boris said. "Most of you will be approaching from their blind side, the fields in the west, with a small advance team going underneath through the tunnel that we have cut through the mountain."

There was a murmur as everyone began conferring about who would be doing what.

"Once the advance team have disabled their defences within, the main teams," Boris went on, "led by Ivan, will make an assault across the fields. Ivan will be leading with our beast here."

Boris signalled to Ivan, a large man in Russian military uniform, who pulled aside an oversized Russian flag, which had been draped over something massive in the middle of the barn. It was a tank—a *huge* tank, bigger than anything Sam had ever seen in a movie or book. The crowd cheered.

"While we attack this facility in Tunguska," Boris said, his voice low and slow as he finished up his pep talk, "our friends all over the country are doing the same, attacking Hypnos centres and strongholds. By tomorrow, my comrades, *we* will be in charge. We will be free!"

The crowd applauded and cheered again, and Boris smiled and stepped off the table, people splintering off into groups.

Sam was with Arianna and Boris, teamed up with the underground assault group. There were eight of them in all, and they assembled in a corner of the barn to crowd around a rudimentary scale model of the Hypnos facility. Sam figured it didn't look imposing or sinister in model form, what with the group of toy men guarding it. There was a main building, with a few smaller ones scattered about, and a tall perimeter fence.

"Before the main assault team attacks with the tank and trucks," Boris said, "we will go through the tunnel here."

He tapped at the back of a rock wall, which looked like a mountain range with the peaks lopped off, towering over the building below.

"What's our objective?" Arianna asked.

"Disable their defences, then we hit the labs," Boris replied. "At the front they will do what they can to keep them occupied, while we evacuate the detainees from these outbuildings."

"What sort of security numbers do they have in there?" Arianna asked.

"We know the Hypnos have only about two dozen guards

here," Boris replied, "and they will likely all be responding to the frontal assault."

"Do they know about this tunnel that we're taking?" Sam asked.

Arianna had to translate into Russian for Boris to understand, and the Russian cop smiled.

"No," he replied. "They don't. Arianna, can you explain to us the labs?"

"From all we've pieced together from those of us who have been experimented on there," Arianna said, "we understand that inside is in two sections. Here," she tapped at the north side of the squat building, "are the medical labs, where they keep those that are currently being implanted with the chips. The south side, here, is the computer and data storage centre."

Something about it wasn't adding up for Sam.

All that data from the dreams is being kept out here? In such a remote area?

He thought back to the Academy's Swiss campus, of Jedi's computer set up.

I guess it can be set up anywhere.

Boris sent the group to go organize their equipment for the operation. Sam and Arianna walked toward the big, open barn door.

"I wonder how the Gear ever got out here to Russia?" Sam said, looking out at the snow-covered field. At the edge of the forest stood tall trees with silver bark and no leaves, and no animals in sight. The tiny farmhouse looked abandoned. The roof was sagging from decades of heavy snowfalls, yet the little chimney spewed puffs of smoke out into the unwelcoming air.

"Where were the Gears made?" Arianna asked.

"Italy or France, we think," Sam replied. "They bear da Vinci's maker's mark, but can't be dated exactly."

"I guess we will know more when I get my dreams back," Arianna said and she motioned toward the farmhouse. "Come, we will use the satellite phone to call your friends."

Sam walked across the field, dirty grey snow crunching underfoot.

As they neared, more of the farmhouse became visible. The little cabin seemed naggingly familiar—a single door and four walls made of solid wood hewn into rough slabs. It was small and never painted, and had a uniform grey and weathered look. No powerline went in. The stump of a chimney still smoked away.

Arianna opened the door and they went inside. Sam stopped just inside the doorway. He took in the heavy solid wooden walls, the little metal fireplace in the middle of the room, the dilapidated kitchen and the single boarded-up window.

He'd been in this place before—he'd dreamed about it.

The cabin in the woods.

ALEX

They'd worked through the night and were finally ready. Alex stood at the controls, Shiva next to him rocking a little side-to-side in some kind of sleep-deprived delirium. Tesla's experimental coil began to vibrate as power started surging through it.

"OK, increasing the power to the coil," Shiva said, and the two of them together leaned on the huge lever.

They stood back and watched. Alex could practically taste the electricity in the room. The noise of the best light show in town bounced around them, the electricity arcing through the dark of the room.

"It seems to be gathering speed!" Alex called out.

The coil lit up from within—a brilliant white-blue hue of electricity running through it.

"It's live!" Shiva yelled over the cacophony. "It's live!"

"Maybe not for much longer!" Alex replied, noticing that the activity seemed to be ebbing. "I think it's running out of juice!"

They watched as the blue light racing around the coil dimmed, the current diminishing, the sound fading.

"She needs more power!" Shiva yelled, reaching for the power lever.

"Shiva, no," Alex said as his friend reached out his hand to the huge power supply lever.

"Hold onto something, taking it to ninety per cent!"

"But Shiva, that's—"

Shiva leaned on the lever, pushing it toward its maximum setting. Sparks erupted from the control panels, then everything went from bright white-blue—

To black. Complete and utter pitch black.

"Too much," Alex gasped.

The whirring echo of the coil powering down rang out around them, the scene in the basement once again lit only by their tiny flashlights.

"No!" Shiva kicked the lever.

WHOMP-WHOMP-WHOMP!

"It's back on!" Alex screamed. "It's coming back online!"

The coil was suddenly lit up like a million Christmas trees, the room around them full of bolts of light.

"This is *amazing!*" Alex said, looking at all the hairs on his bare forearms standing on end. Then he noticed Shiva's black mop of hair standing at full attention.

"Ha!" Alex said, pointing at him. "You look like a toilet brush!"

"You too!"

Alex felt his head, which had gone full afro.

"What happens now?" Alex said over the noise.

"We power down!" Shiva said.

"*What?*" Alex tried cupping his hands around his ears to hear Shiva over the noise.

"This was just for proof of the concept, to see if the coil still worked!" Shiva said, wrestling with the controls. "We can't harness the Dreamscape with what we have here."

"But—"

"No buts, it's too dangerous to go any further," Shiva said, his face strained with effort. "Help me with this lever."

The pair of them pulled at the lever. It didn't budge at all.

"Pull!" Alex said. "Harder!"

Their feet on the panel, all hands on the lever, they heaved with all their weight.

The lever handle snapped off.

"We'll have to cut the powerlines!" Shiva said. He reached for the cables and was thrown back across the room as bolts of lightning sparked all around him.

Shiva!

Alex rushed over to check his friend's vital signs—he was out cold and his hair was singed, but his heart was beating.

Phew.

Shiva had the biggest grin stuck on his face like he thought he'd just pulled the greatest trick.

Typical. What a nerd.

Alex turned back to the machine but the stump of what

was left of the lever was locked on full power. He looked around the room, now fully illuminated by the piercing light arcing from the Tesla coils.

A glint from the far wall caught his gaze. It was a fire axe.

He hefted it at the lever's remains but it was no use, it wasn't going to power down that way. The thick snaking power line was at his feet.

"Ah, the hell with it . . ." Alex said, and brought the axe over his head and swung at the powerline with every ounce of strength he had.

The line sliced in two as Alex was blown across the room by the force of the electric shock.

As Alex blacked out, he caught one fleeting glimpse of the world outside above him through a tiny window. The power was going out.

31

SAM

"What's wrong?" Arianna asked.

"It's . . . déjà vu. You know?"

"Sure, but what's giving you déjà vu right now? Something you dreamed?"

"This place. This room. I've been here before, with you," he said. "Talking, like this. But it was nighttime, and the wolves came—"

"Wolves?"

"Yeah."

"There are no wolves around here."

"Really?"

"OK, I am not completely sure. It is possible. But I think the farmers would keep them away."

Sam watched the crackling fire behind the steel grill.

"We sat right here . . ." Sam said. "You, me, this place—"

"The phone's not here," Arianna interrupted.

"Sorry?"

"The satellite phone, it's gone."

"Someone must be using it," Sam said. He walked to the boarded-up window and peered out through a tiny crack to the dull grey world outside. He thought he saw movement, white against the white, but no, it was nothing.

"Argh!" Arianna cried out.

"What is it?" Sam said, helping her sit down in a chair.

"My head . . ." Arianna said. "It's like a migraine. But it just started now."

"I'll get you some water," Sam said, turning on the tap. No water came out. "The pipes must be frozen."

"*Argh!*" Arianna screamed, clutching at her head. "Something's . . . happening!"

Sam raced to the door to get help. He pulled at the handle—the door wouldn't move.

Then, the whole building did. They were *moving*.

"It's a trap!" Sam yelled. He peered through the slim gap between the window boards.

The entire cabin was straining and heaving, but unmistakably moving—*on the back of a truck*, Sam guessed. He could make out outlines of white moving in the farm-land beyond, men in Stealth Suits, effortlessly darting the Nyx, most of whom were like Arianna was now, crouched down in pain, their hands on their heads.

The chips. They've triggered something in their implanted chips.

"It'll be OK," Sam murmured to Arianna, holding her tight, staring at the locked door ahead as the cabin rumbled on beneath them. "It'll be OK," he said, knowing that it wouldn't.

Sam struggled against the restraints rubbing against his wrists. It had been two hours since they'd gone into that wooden cabin, where he'd been locked inside with Arianna and transported. Now they were in the Tunguska Dreamer facility.

Not how we planned to be here.

"We really must stop meeting like this," Hans said to Sam. "You see, it was obvious that you'd come here," Hans said. "That's why I sowed the seed about her dreams in Moscow."

"What are you talking about?" Arianna said. "You could not have known about us coming here."

Hans laughed.

Sam looked around—he was in a dentist-type chair, his arms and legs and neck and forehead strapped down tight. Arianna sat opposite, tied to a metal office chair. Hans was wearing a lab coat, as were the seven technicians Sam could see moving around in his line of vision. It was a small room with only a handful of computers and some shelves stacked with clear plastic tubs. There was, however, plenty of medical gear in sight.

Not good . . .

I need to buy as much time as I can. Implanting the dream chip is risky . . . they won't chance it with me, will they?

"You and your Hypnos will never succeed," Sam said.

"Well, I never said they were *my* Hypnos, and one could

argue that they've already succeeded," Hans said. "You see, with their technology and your dreams, there will soon be a new world order. Sounds enticing, doesn't it, Sam?"

"Is this all because you've got an inferiority complex because you're short?" Sam jeered, playing for time.

"Ah, Sam, you kill me, really," Hans chortled.

"Given the chance, yeah." Sam couldn't help himself.

Hans chuckled. "Always with fight in you. I like it."

"If you're involved with the atrocities that have happened here," Sam said, "you'll pay for that."

"Atrocities? I'm doing my role to be sure that I am the victor—I'm not the bad guy, Sam. I'm not Solaris."

"Solaris didn't attack me in Denver!" Sam said.

"Ah, yes," Hans said. "That was most unusual. Really makes you think, doesn't it?"

Sam was puzzled and Hans could read that.

"I see that you've been wondering about it too . . ." Hans said. "Think about it. Why would he save you, Sam? Why save you, only to send you away?"

"Probably so we could have this little play date here," Sam said, subtly working against his bindings. He could see that Arianna was doing the same.

"Or," Hans said, "perhaps it is because you are working together? That would be quite a twist, don't you think?"

"Maybe I *am* Solaris," Sam said. "Ever think of that?"

Hans shook his head. "I'm trying to be reasonable here,

Sam. Solaris could do as we were doing," he said. "As we will continue to do."

Sam knew what that meant—read his dreams, steal them and keep him captive. Have him in some kind of stasis until all thirteen Gears were found.

"You see," Hans said, nodding to a technician who tapped at a syringe and then moved toward Sam, the clear liquid-filled needle slicing into his arm with a sharp jab. Sam glared at the technician, straining to pull his arm away but it was no use.

"I knew that when I said that your dream led me to Arianna, and hers then to the Gear," Hans continued, "that you would think of coming here first, to, ah, attempt to get her dreams back. Am I right?"

"Must get annoying," Sam said, cringing as the needle was pulled out. "Always being right."

"Sarcasm suits you, Sam," Hans said. "You should keep it up."

"Sure, why not?" Sam said. "I get lots of practice, having met you enough times."

Hans' eyes narrowed as he chuckled to himself. "We found the cabin and had it dismantled and remade onto the back of a truck," he said. "The rest, you two did. It was just too easy. It's almost like you wanted to be caught."

Sam's vision started to blur.

"Ah, there it is," Hans said, walking closer to Sam. "Your familiar friend in that syringe. You'll be dreaming soon

Sam, and the more you dream, the less you are going to remember. But don't worry, *I* won't miss a thing. Come now, why don't you sleep for us? Show me who the next Dreamer is."

Sam grimaced as the drug took hold.

Hans nodded to the technician behind Sam, and he could hear a buzzing sound start up.

"I'll give you this last chance," Hans said quietly, so close to Sam that he could smell his oily breath. "Join me, or suffer like your friend Arianna here. Look at her. So pretty, so special, yet she will never remember her own dreams."

Sam looked across to Arianna. Silent tears streamed down her face. Sam's vision clouded and his head rolled back, his eyes closing.

"We don't have to do this, Sam," Hans said. "Save yourself the headaches. Choose to keep your dreams. Say you'll join me, just say it."

Sam felt himself slipping into unconsciousness.

"Say it," Hans said.

Sam's lips moved, and Hans leaned in to listen.

"Never . . ."

EVA

"**Z**odiac signs in astrology, the ones we know, like Pisces, Sagittarius et cetera—are all thirty degrees in length," Jedi said, "to make the full three-sixty degree orbit that the sun makes in a year. But the actual constellations, the star patterns that they refer to, vary in size."

"OK, I'm with you so far," Eva said.

"Having those convenient boundaries was helpful for astronomers, but along with the twelve constellations, there is a thirteenth," Jedi continued. "It was more recently called Ophiuchus, known as the 'serpent bearer.'"

"So while the world finds it easy to follow the twelve divisions of the zodiac—twelve months of the year, divided into four seasons and so on, there is this other, thirteenth part that has always been there," Lora added.

"And I guess that number's pretty important for us, huh?" Eva said.

"Exactly," the Professor said. "We have come too far to imagine that such a dream from you is not significant."

"So where is this zodiac," Eva asked, "this disc that I dreamed of?"

"That, we don't yet know," the Professor said. "We'd never seen this particular image before your dream last night."

"What if it doesn't exist?" Eva said. "Or what if it's lost forever?"

"Hopefully that's not the case," Lora said, "and we have reason to be hopeful. Dr. Dark's team found mention of Ophiuchus, which falls between Scorpio and Sagittarius, several times in their research."

"It would appear that we must look into it more," the Professor said.

"All because I dreamed about it?" Eva said.

"Yes," the Professor replied.

"But . . . I'm pleased you have such confidence in me but we don't even know for sure if—"

"Eva, the first thing we teach students here," the Professor said with a friendly smile, "is to follow their dreams."

"Yes, I know . . ." Eva said.

"Dr. Dark is on his way here," Lora said. "He will guide you through your dream, and will accompany you to find this zodiac. It seems too crucial now to ignore and it may add to our knowledge of the Dream Gate."

"What about finding Sam?" Eva said. "What about the Dreamer competition? There's so much for us to do . . ."

"We will not stop doing all we can to find Sam," Lora said. "And as for the Dreamer Doors, let the others worry about that. You have an important job to do."

"OK," Eva said. "Wow."

So I do have a bigger part to play in the race. I hope I'm up to it . . .

"Don't underestimate yourself, Eva," the Professor said, uncannily perceiving her thoughts. "You are a powerful Dreamer. And you must dare to dream, and follow your dreams."

SAM'S DREAM

I stretch out against my sleepiness as the morning sunshine spills across my face.

I sit up in bed and look out of my bedroom window, down at the green fields of the Academy's campus outside London.

The sun is peering through wispy white clouds, the light and warmth drawing out the students to play sports and games. There is some sort of tournament coming up. They all look so happy.

I smile.

I know what Hans is doing. I gotta stay calm.

I pick up my tablet and flick to the Academy's home-page, reading the latest newsletter.

There is a short clip of me arriving back from Russia, via helicopter, being mobbed by hundreds of jubilant students, then I am lofted into the air and carried back to the main hall, where the video file stops on a close-up of me holding up the lanyard with the four Gears. Cheers ring out.

Is this my subconsious having fun with me? I guess it's my ultimate dream come true . . .

The Echo
The Academy Newsletter

THE
ACADEMY
mens agitat molem

Issue 26

SAM'S DONE IT AGAIN!

Sam has returned from another adventure abroad, where
he met the seventh known Dreamer, Cody, of Arizona.
Working with Cody, Sam managed to, yet again, overcome
overwhelming odds to come up trumps and get to the next
Gear before our enemies. The Academy is currently
in possession of six of the precious Gears, two remain with
Solaris. Sam is currently recuperating at the Academy and
staff ask that students respect his privacy as he prepares to

A knock at the door rouses me.

"Yeah?" I say.

The door inches open and a smiling face appears.

"Eva!" I say, rushing to her and hugging her.

*This is good, keep the dream neutral. Don't give away
anything.*

"How are you feeling?" she asks, revealing that she's
brought with her a trolley laden with breakfast.

"Fine—wait, no, better than fine!" I say, jumping around
the room. "I'm ready to conquer the world!"

Eva laughs. "Can't do it on an empty stomach. Clear off
your desk and I'll set up."

I make space by stacking up the books and papers,

pausing as I see Dr. Kader's leather-bound notebook. I pick it up, its worn and beaten appearance jogging something just out of grasp in my memory.

"What is it?" Eva asks, looking at the notebook after placing a covered plate on the desk in front of me.

Don't think about it . . . concentrate on Eva, food, anything.

"I . . . I'm not . . . it's nothing," I say, putting the notebook aside. "What's for breakfast?"

"Guess," Eva says.

"Hmm . . ." my hand hovers over one of the stainless steel covers. "Smells like . . . bacon. Bacon, scrambled eggs and buttered toast. And mushrooms!"

"Maybe. Have a look."

I lift the lid.

"Ha, exactly what I guessed!"

"Tea or coffee?" Eva asks.

"Juice."

She pours orange juice from a jug, two glasses.

I sit on the edge of my bed, the plate of food on my lap, Eva at my desk.

"So," Eva says after I start eating. "Tell me about your last mission."

I finish my mouthful and have a sip of juice. Eva seems to mirror my moves.

Uh-oh. They're in here too.

"What do you want to know?" I say slowly.

Eva smiles. "Tell me everything."

"Well," I say, then look at her, and she looks at me. I eat another forkful of egg on toast—she does too. "It all started in Arizona . . ."

"And then you went with Cody to Colorado?" Eva asks.

"Yep," I say.

"What did you see there, in Denver?"

"What's with you and the fifty questions this morning?" I say.

"Just curious." Eva smiles, waiting for my reply.

I'll bet.

"OK," I say, putting my empty plate on the tray, then taking Eva's and stacking it. "Well, you and Lora were headed there too, right?"

"Right."

"Where'd you guys end up?"

"We—we were nearly there, but had to stop."

"OK, well, let's see, Denver . . . Denver. Oh, I was with Cody, after we'd been to the temple in the Grand Canyon."

They know this already. This is OK. Keep talking about what's already happened. Stay away from the future.

"What did you find there?"

"The next Gear."

"Oh." Eva's face seems frozen by the idea.

"But we were kind of double-crossed by Cody's parents."

"Enterprise Agents?" Eva asks.

"Yeah," I say, leaning by the window. It is empty out there

now, no students in sight. The sun was still out, the clouds too, but not moving—there mustn't be a breath of air at all.

Is this because I'm steering the dream or is this them?

"Wait," I say, looking at Eva, who stands and backs away. I do a double take. "What am I saying?"

"Huh? What's wrong?"

"I just realized—Cody's parents weren't working for the Enterprise, they were working with Mac."

"Oh." Eva seems to settle and joins me by the window. "Mac?"

"Yeah, that American guy, the one who betrayed the Dreamer Council in Paris?"

Eva nods.

"Well, he also worked for the US government, and he took us to some kind of base under Denver Airport. The Ark? I think they called it the Central Ark."

"Called what the Central Ark?"

"The place, it was designed as some kind of doomsday bunker—"

"What happened in Denver?" Eva interrupts.

Damn. Concentrate, stop telling her stuff she doesn't already know. Fight it, Sam, fight it.

I squint, looking outside. It's still dead silent out there. I look at a couple of birds in the sky, little specks of black against the grey. They don't move. Two still dots. The wisps of cloud are still, not moving across the sky at all.

"Sam?"

"I, ahhh . . ."

"Sam, look at me."

I look at Eva, my friend from the start, always there for me.

Betraying me now. But it's not really her.

"Mac wasn't working for the government anymore," I say.

Fight it!

Eva's expression turns serious. "Who was he working for?"

I look back at those motionless birds in the sky.

"Solaris was there," I say.

"What did he want?"

"To save me."

"How'd he save you?"

I look from her to the floor.

"I don't think he did."

When I look back up, Eva is gone.

I stand in my room. An empty room—dull, as grey as the sky outside had been, lifeless. Even the window is just a few painted lines on a concrete wall.

34

ALEX

Alex woke up in a familiar setting.

A hospital.

A hospital he'd been in before.

The door opened. Two cops walked in—one an older guy with no hair, the other a younger one with a wide grin.

He'd seen them before too.

"So, if it isn't our little terrorist friend," the older cop said to Alex.

"Found at the site of another explosion in our fine city," his colleague added.

"With an accomplice this time."

"Oh great, these guys again . . ." Alex said under his breath as he leaned back onto the pillow and looked up at the ceiling.

How'd I get here? More importantly, how do I get out?

"Seems our Federal friends from last time didn't teach you a lesson," the older one continued.

"Maybe you're just a little slow to catch on. Do you remember us, sonny? I'm Detective Carter," the younger one said. "And this here is Detective Montrose."

"When we heard it was you," Montrose said, "we just had to come by to say hi."

"And this time," Carter said, "we ain't gonna let you out of our sight."

"Feds?" Alex said. "Are you really so incompetent that you failed to realize last time that those weren't Feds? Nope. You handed me straight over to the bad guys."

Alex sat up and saw that the two cops looked a little uneasy.

"That's right," Alex said, getting out of the bed and standing a little unsteadily on his feet. "You two handed me over to a team of Agents that weren't Federal *anything*— they were the ones you were after, *they* were the ones who caused that explosion."

They remained silent, trading glances, then Montrose said, "And this last explosion, in downtown Manhattan, I guess you weren't involved in that either?"

Well, it's not like we meant it.

"Where's my friend, Shiva?"

"Shiva?" Carter said, his eyebrows raised. "What's that, your friend's name? Had a different name in his passport."

"What's yours?" Montrose said, sniggering. "No, wait, lemme guess—Zeus?"

"It's his online handle . . ." Alex said, the feeling coming back into his legs now. He had small grazes on his hands that stung but apart from that he felt fine. "His name's Rahul. Where is he?"

"Online handle?"

"You guys some kind of hackers?"

"You trying to hack into City Hall?"

"You trying to steal our paycheques? Our pensions?"

"Now we're talking a serious felony."

"Serious."

"*Long* jail time."

"Real long I bet. Fifteen years?"

"Least. Maybe twenty."

The cops whistled as though in awe at their own little sideshow.

Alex shook his head with exasperation.

"Look, guys, just tell me," Alex said, "is my friend OK?"

The two cops looked to each other and shrugged.

"Yeah, he's down the hall," Montrose said.

"As OK as a criminal can be," Carter added, with a chuckle on top. "Are terrorists regarded as mere criminals?" he asked his partner in mock seriousness.

"Nope, they're *far* worse," Montrose said. "The worst."

"Listen," Alex said to Carter. "Maybe we can work something out here and clear up this innocent mess . . ."

"You think this is an innocent mess?" Montrose said. "We've got an old building downtown all messed up and the whole lower half of Manhattan was blacked out after your little stunt."

"I thought it was a brownout," Carter replied.

"Whatever," Montrose said, "this is serious."

"*Real* serious. This is the second time we've linked your whereabouts to the location of a massive explosion."

"We ain't gonna wait around for a third time."

"No chance."

"So how about you start talkin', kid."

"OK . . ." Alex said, sorting through the thoughts in his mind. "How about this? You help us, I'll help you," he said. "I can get you the names and details of who was responsible for the explosion the last time we met. You'll get promotions, and medals, I'm sure. We give you the names, you check them out. You think I'm lying, you can arrest me. What you got to lose? Nothing. But think about what you've got to gain when you take down some really big players in the criminal world. Cross my heart. Just make a call to my mother, her name's Phoebe, she'll tell you everything."

"Your *mother*? Are you freaking kidding?"

Alex shook his head. "Nuh-uh, I'm for real."

They looked at each other, then shrugged again.

"Fine," Carter said. "But you double-cross us on this, you won't be seeing daylight for the next few decades. You *and* your buddy, Rahul."

"Trust me," Alex said, smiling. "Just you wait and see, you guys are gonna be heroes."

SAM'S DREAM

I take off the visor that is strapped around my head. It has a little antenna, transmitting wirelessly to some-place outside the room. I look through the visor screen, but it is clear now.

I look around the room. Grey concrete blocks, a single bed and a painted-on window. There is also a heavy steel door.

It's a cell.

But where? The underground lab in Denver?

No.

I can easily see that this place is older and less maintained.

What's the last thing I can remember?

As much as I try, I draw a blank.

I'm wearing a dark blue prison-like jumpsuit.

They took my Stealth Suit?

I tiptoe across to the door and listen.

There are footsteps. They are coming closer.

And voices, but not speaking in English.

Russian?

I back away from the door—

It opens.

A man and a woman in lab coats stand in the doorway. They enter the room without speaking. The woman takes my virtual-reality visor while the man checks my heart rate, blood pressure, and shines a small light into my eyes.

"One hundred and ten over seventy, pupil dilation back to normal," the man says in English, and the woman jots it down on a notepad along with the time that she gets from a thin gold watch around her wrist. The man seems familiar in some way.

I touch my chest, where the brass Gears should be—nothing.

"Welcome back to the waking world, Sam," the man says. "I am Demetri, head of the Russian Dreamer Program."

"Where am I?"

"A secure location, for observation."

"How'd I get here?"

"You fell from the sky."

"I—what?"

Demetri smiles. "Come, I'll show you. Hopefully it will jog your memory so that you can tell us how you came to be here with us."

Wait a minute, this happened already. I don't remember it, but it did.

I'm still in a dream.

Right, time to mess with them.

What I see more resembles the space launch control room of the Apollo missions from the 1960s that I've studied in class than any kind of modern scientific endeavour.

"Here," Demetri says, his hand gesturing to a seat in a small theatre-like room. "Take a seat."

I sit.

Demetri motions to a technician who starts up the projector.

"Our sensors detected an unidentified object flying through a suborbital trajectory across our night sky, vectoring to pass directly over this installation."

I watch the footage of a bright burning mass in the night sky, taking me back to another science class when we watched magnified images of comets streaming through space.

"That's me?" I ask.

"You are inside. This footage was still some two hundred kilometres west of here. We scrambled two fighter jets to take a closer look at your pod."

The images change to what must be video footage from the jets. It is impossible to judge the size of the pod but one thing is clear—it is travelling fast.

"Our jets quickly ran out of fuel trying to keep up with your speed, and it was decided by our central command that whatever you were, you were a threat to our airspace."

"What does that mean?"

"It means, I'm sorry to say, that our nation's air defences shot you down."

"Shot me down?" I say. "Like, out of the sky?"

Wow. Maybe this part's true?

Demetri nods and points at the screen.

It is vision from a new angle. There is the bright light of my pod, hurtling along, then a tiny bright arrow streaking up from below—the collision inevitable.

The impact makes me jump in my seat. A huge fireball engulfs the pod and it immediately changes direction, shedding debris in its wake as it loses altitude.

Images of Sebastian being shot out of the sky by a missile in New York flash through my mind—the flaming wreckage crashing to earth. I swallow hard to stop the rising bile in my throat.

Don't get emotional. Stay neutral.

"Here we have the impact as captured by yet another angle. You can see in the early morning dawn that this footage was taken from a helicopter."

My pod is now a steaming hulk the size of a delivery van, driven hard into a snow-covered expanse of earth, the gouge in the ground from the initial impact a couple of kilometres long.

"At first, the military was going through ridiculous celebrations," Demetri says. "They thought that Superman had landed—that he exists, and that he will be Russian!"

Demetri laughs but I just watch in shock as the footage now shows the President of Russia inspecting the crash site.

"When I arrived with my team and analyzed the site, we found that it was in fact a rocket capsule made in America, for their Ark program," Demetri says. "It's a fall-back site for their government, in the event of an all-out nuclear war. We have a similar program here. After breaching the hull and finding that it only contained you, and following a lot of tests, we managed to take over your observation as you safely recovered."

The Ark? Did they find out about that from me?

They'll say anything to trick me into giving them information.

"Recovered?"

"You sustained a head injury on impact," Demetri says.

I feel the back of my head—it is shaved, and I can feel stitches running along a vertical scar.

I didn't have a scar.

"You slipped in and out of consciousness a few times," Demetri explains, "and I suspect that you may have loss of some memory function."

"When was this?" I ask. "When did this accident—this shooting-down of the pod, happen?"

"A week ago."

"A week?" I say. "I've been here for a week?"

"More or less."

"I need to call . . ." I look blankly into middle distance.

"Who?"

"I don't know," I say. "I don't remember. Someone. Someone is worried about me. I'm sure of it."

Demetri smiles. "It will come back, trust me. First, tell me, do you remember why Solaris put you in that pod?"

I shake my head.

Demetri's smile remains unchanged.

"That is unfortunate," he says. "Why don't you close your eyes a moment and think about it?"

I close my eyes. My world goes dark.

EVA

D r. Dark's private jet was waiting on the wet tarmac at London's Heathrow Airport.

"You can't come?" Eva asked Lora as they exited the private terminal and walked toward the jet.

"No," she said, "it's better for me to stay and direct our efforts from here."

"You'll tell me if you find anything about Sam?" Eva said.

"Of course," Lora said, hugging her. As they embraced, she passed her a wrapped package. "Open it in private."

"What is it?"

"Something that you may need. Be safe out there, and remember to be careful who you trust."

Eva looked at her oddly but Lora waved her off and made her way back to the terminal. Eva slipped the parcel into her backpack and walked toward Dr. Dark, who was waiting for her at the entrance to the plane.

"Eva, good to see you again," he said.

"Where are we headed?" she asked, going up the stairs.

"First stop, New York City," he replied as they got out of the drizzle and into the warm cabin. A crew member poured coffee. "We take off in five minutes, we're just waiting for another passenger. Make yourself comfortable."

Eva helped herself to a plush leather chair that was more comfortable than her bed back at the Academy.

"How's my son getting on?" Dr. Dark asked.

"Good," Eva replied, putting her backpack at her feet. "He's a gifted Dreamer, though he's taken Sam's disappearance quite hard."

"Yes, it's messy, but we'll find him," Dr. Dark said. "The two boys were classmates in high school, so Xavier's bound to be more affected by it than most."

Not as much as me.

"So," Eva said, "Why New York as our first stop?"

"Well, I watched the recording of your last dream," Dr. Dark said, "and since the thirteen zodiac tablet you saw appears to be Ancient Egyptian, I think we should start with my research team's archives. I had them moved from Berlin to New York."

"You think we'll find answers there?"

"Possibly, it's worth a try," he said, sipping his coffee. "But ultimately, there's only one way that we can see into every mind on the planet to really know everything for sure."

"Every mind?"

"Yes, via their dreams."

"No one can do that."

"Maybe not, but I think there may well be a way," Dr. Dark said with a cryptic smile.

He handed over a black leather-bound book.

It was heavy, with thick, cream pages. Eva opened the cover.

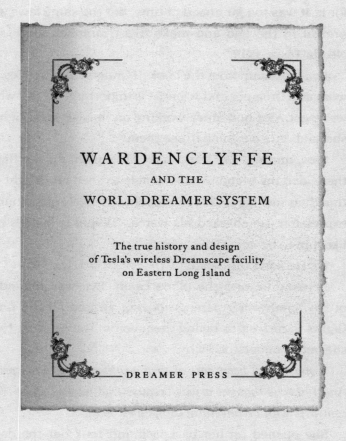

WARDENCLYFFE

AND THE

WORLD DREAMER SYSTEM

The true history and design
of Tesla's wireless Dreamscape facility
on Eastern Long Island

DREAMER PRESS

There was a notation on the next page. Eva read it out loud to herself.

"The tower was destroyed two years ago but my

projects are being developed and another one, improved in some features, will be constructed . . . My project was retarded by laws of nature. The world was not prepared for it. It was too far ahead of time, but the same laws will prevail in the end and make it a triumphal success—Nikola Tesla, 1919."

Eva looked up from the book. "I understand that Tesla's work as a Dreamer and scientist is important—that's what we've got Alex and Shiva working on in New York, right?" she said. "Are we going to see them?"

"Yes, and no," Dr. Dark said. "I'll explain on the flight there, and my friend should be able to shed more light on this than me," he added in response to Eva's questioning expression. He checked his watch. "Where is he? It's not like him to be late. I'll just check."

Dr. Dark left the cabin.

Looking around the plane cabin, Eva was reminded of her family—her parents moving around all the time, flights to new cities taking them across the country. Now she better understood why.

It must have been part of their work with the Enterprise. And I always thought it was because Dad worked short-term contracts with architectural companies. Huh.

She opened up her backpack and took out the day's paper she'd picked up as she'd walked through the terminal minutes before. The front page headline made her heart skip a beat, and she read it slowly.

DAILY NEWS

World · Business · Finance · Lifestyle · Travel · Sport · Weather

Issue: 240104   THE WORLDS BEST SELLING NATIONAL NEWSPAPER   Est - 1965

First Edition

EXPLOSION IN BASEMENT IN DOWNTOWN MANHATTAN

Police questioned two young men who were found by paramedics at the scene of an explosion in a basement in Manhattan. One is believed to be involved in the dramatic plane crash in Manhattan several weeks ago. Somehow, he and his unnamed accomplice escaped police custody while recovering in hospital.

His whereabouts are currently unknown, but the government, along with attendees at a special meeting of the United Nations Security Council have described this individual as highly suspicious and are eager to question him immediately.

Anyone with any information regarding these suspects should call the Federal police number given below. Members of the public are urged not to approach these men as they could be armed and dangerous.

Eva swallowed hard.

She folded up the paper and put it into her bag.

Alex and Shiva are in New York, and we're going there now. We can help them.

Then we just need to find Sam and it'll be the three of us again. Like it was at the beginning.

Looking outside the window, she saw a man walking with a limp toward Dr. Dark.

The two embraced like old friends. She heard the engines of the jet powering up for takeoff. She looked at Lora's gift in her bag and tore the end open. There was a box.

Inside, Eva was surprised to find a dart gun, standard Enterprise Agent issue. The information with it stated it was accurate to fifty metres and could render a person unconscious for anywhere from an hour to a full day. There were sixty darts in the box. She zipped up her bag, pulling it closer to her.

Dr. Dark stepped into the cabin once more. The other man was close behind. He had an open, friendly face and with his round glasses, beard and rumpled clothes, he gave off the air of a teacher or scholar. He reminded Eva of Tobias, just a little older.

"Eva, this is a good friend of mine, Dr. Ahmed Kader," Dr. Dark said smoothly.

What!

That traitor.

Eva struggled to smile and muttered out a mumbled greeting as she leaned forward and threw back the zip on her bag. Pulling out the box, she reached inside it and in one fluid movement she leapt to her feet. She raised the dart gun level to point it right at Dr. Kader.

"He was in Denver with Mac—he betrayed us all," Eva said through gritted teeth. "How could you?"

"Eva, you don't—" Dr. Dark said.

"I'm not going anywhere with this man!" Eva shouted. "I'm getting off this plane—*right now.*"

37

"**P**hoebe *really* managed to get those cops to let us go?" Shiva said as they walked down the corridor to Shiva's apartment in New York.

"She can be very convincing," Alex said. "Besides, the files she gave them on Stella and Matrix are huge and will keep them busy. And with any luck, they'll arrest the pair of them so that they're out of this race long enough for us to get to the Dream Gate."

"You know, I always thought your mum was cool," Shiva said, "but now she's made my all-time favourite people board."

"I'll be sure to let her know that," Alex said. "Hey, are you sure you're OK? Maybe you should have gotten some crutches at the hospital?"

"What? This little leg thing?" Shiva said, pointing down as he limped along next to Alex. "Nah, I'll be fine. Give me a day or two and I'll be back on my board."

Alex laughed as they walked into Shiva's home. "Whoa. *This* is your place?" he said, looking around the big open-plan apartment. They were in a Brooklyn suburb, just across the East River. Alex turned to look back to the twinkling lights of Manhattan's skyline.

"Yep," Shiva replied, kicking back on a couch with his legs up. "Used to live here until the Enterprise recruited me last year. Now it's more of a weekender, though my brother seems to crash here a lot."

"Some weekender, it's so cool!" Alex replied, walking around the expansive space and taking it in. To one side of the main room stood a table tennis table, next to consoles and massive screens and a mini indoor golf driving range. A couple of basketball hoops were at either end of the room, while at the front floor-to-ceiling windows was a custom-made half-pipe with grind bars along the window sills for skating. "You weren't joking about boarding, eh? And you got all *this* from skimming money out of criminals' bank accounts?"

"Yep. A few cents here and there across thousands of accounts daily, all adds up. Plus I do get paid a pretty nice salary at the Enterprise. I don't work there for free, you know."

"Nice work, man," Alex said. "So, getting back to business, how'd you think that Tesla—"

"My recording device!" Shiva exclaimed, sitting bolt upright.

"What about it?"

"I forgot—it's back at the site, we have to go and get it!"

"That place has been cordoned off by the cops," Alex said.

"Then we'll have to break in!" Shiva pulled himself up and hobbled for the door. "Come on—and you'll have to drive!"

He tossed Alex a set of keys and together they went to the basement parking garage via the elevator.

The car Shiva stopped beside was a midnight blue high-performance sports car.

"Is this . . . ?" Alex stuttered, pointing at the car.

"Yes, it is," Shiva replied. "A Tesla Roadster, totally electric. I believe in my work, what can I tell you?"

"That's impressive, man! But you, ah, sure you want me to drive? I only just got my probationary licence."

"Sure—just try not to scratch it," Shiva said as Alex helped him into the passenger seat. "I'm kidding, but seriously, don't scratch it."

"Man, this is a sweet ride," Alex said, adjusting the seat and steering wheel. "If I didn't know you as a Robin Hood hacker type, I'd wonder how a no-good cyber bum like you managed to have all this."

"I like to think of myself as a cyber punk."

"A what?"

"A high-tech low-life," Shiva explained with a grin.

Alex laughed, started the car and drove up the ramp. "How'd you find out about all this Tesla stuff?" Alex said. "I mean, it seems as though the Council and Academy, and even your bosses at the Enterprise, turned their back on it ages ago."

"I cracked a code a while back," Shiva said as he pressed

a button to open the garage door. "No one at the Enterprise believed me, so I did it all from here. Took three years, but I cracked it."

"Code to what?" Alex said, creeping the car forward as the garage door slowly tilted up.

"A group in Eastern Europe who have been working on the Tesla Wave angle for the past hundred years," Shiva said. "They're known as the Hypnos, and I've been tracking their progress ever since."

"Why don't the Enterprise and Academy do anything about them?"

"They've got their own problems. Rather, had. The entire world's going to have to come together on this race to the Dream Gate, right? I mean, these guys have tech that we've forgotten about—but it's going to come in handy."

Alex thought back to the front page of the *New York Times* which had shown the downed aircraft from the last time he'd been in this city.

Yeah, we've all been busy.

As the garage door clunked fully open, Alex put the car in gear and accelerated to climb the exit ramp to the street.

And stopped.

Blocking their path were a couple of big, black SUVs—an effective road block.

Beside the cars stood several people, waiting for them. With the blinding sunlight behind them, they cast long silhouettes.

"Oh no . . ." Shiva said as Alex gasped in shock, recognizing the two who walked forward as soon as Shiva did—it was Stella and Matrix, and they weren't making a friendly house call.

SAM

Sam woke to find himself in another blank room, this time someplace distinctly dank and eerie.

Underground.

One eye opened first. It took in a grey room full of dull light. It closed again for a few minutes. The image of a blue sky flitted across his mind. He heard laughter, the sun was warm on his face.

Nice dream.

Wishful thinking.

Wake up, Sam. Open your eyes.

His eyes fluttered open.

He saw a machine straight ahead of him. An outdated mess of switches and lights and dials on a military-grey box along with a few new add-ons that suggested laptop computers. A thick bunch of cables went under the door.

He sat up. He was in a bed, starched sheets wrapped around him.

There was nothing much else in the room, only bare concrete walls, an IV drip connected into his arm and a heart-rate monitor on a wheeled stand. Some small screens bleeped next to him while control panels on the larger machine at the other side of his bed looked like they were charting his sleep patterns.

Every now and then the heart-rate monitor bleeped, and the big boxy machine whirred and whacked out of sync every time he . . . thought.

What?

He reached up to feel his head and flinched when he touched a rubber skullcap. He turned to see it was connected by wires to the machine next to him. In the near complete silence all Sam could hear was the faint whir of a ducted fan above him and the rhythmic beeps of the machines.

Thoughts . . . that machine is recording my thoughts, awake and asleep. My brain waves.

He was wearing a hospital gown.

Think. Where am I?

There was a door with a little wire-mesh window set in at eye level. No cameras that Sam could see. The room seemed old—the damp stains in the concrete walls where it met the floor suggested it had been built a long time ago.

You know where you are, Sam. Control your mind. Think about the past, don't give anything away.

OK, the Dreamer, Cody, back at . . . where? The Grand Canyon. That was it. An old temple. The Gears—

He instinctively touched at his neck where a leather strap had been under his T-shirt.

Gone.

Ahmed took the Gears . . . Dr. Kader, Xavier's godfather, working with—

The US government.

No.

Mac. He went outside the government. A senior member of the Dreamer Council, who was he working for . . . ?

Solaris.

Solaris was there. In Denver.

Denver. The flash of light—

Stop it, Sam! Think of something else . . .

I can't, I can't, my mind wants to go there.

Imagine a different story . . . tell them something else.

"The nuke is going to detonate!" Sam said, suddenly more awake than ever as he fought to create a false trail, a lie that Hans could believe. Yes, he'd been in the bunker deep below Denver airport, Mac's lair, when Solaris had crashed the party. A self-destruct mechanism *had* been set off.

The big grey machine was all lit up now, lights and dials flashing and twirling.

Now what?

The bomb was up on the surface, it would take out the airport and most of the surrounding area. Solaris tried to stop the countdown . . . to save me. The countdown skipped ahead.

The last thing I saw was the timer. It read six minutes.

Then . . . then there was a flash and that was it.

The countdown stopped with one second to go . . .

"Come with me!" Solaris said, and we ran through a dark corridor, the red warning lights were flashing, there was a line of hatch-like doors. Solaris tapped away at a control panel, entering latitude and longitude.

"FOUR MINUTES TO SELF DESTRUCT . . ." echoed through the alarm system.

"Until next time!" Solaris had said, pushing me into the capsule.

"Where are you sending me?" I'd asked.

"Where you need to go."

"Why?"

Solaris had paused. "We're two of a kind, Sam. One cannot live without the other," he told me.

"THREE MINUTES TO SELF DESTRUCT . . ."

Solaris closed the door. I sat back. It was like a capsule. I strapped in, pulling the harness belts over my shoulders.

In the middle of the floor was a digital screen with the countdown.

2:58

2:57

2:56

Next to the screen was a flashing box that took up most of the space.

TOUCH TO LAUNCH

I touched my foot on the square—

TOUCH TO CONFIRM LAUNCH

I tapped again—

There was an immediate burst of thrust that pushed me down into the seat as the escape pod shot up, the G-forces so great that I blacked out within a second.

And now I'm here, in this room.

Wherever here is . . . trapped.

That's enough!

Sam ripped the skull cap off and ran at the door to bang on it.

"Somebody!" he called. "Help!"

He called out like that again and again, until his voice gave out. He went back to the bed, his head aching, his mind tired. He sat on the edge of the bed, clutching at his head as a sharp pain seemed to cut into it like a splitting headache.

Sam took in a slow, deep breath as the reality came flooding back to him again.

I'm in the lab at Tunguska, Russia. Hans tricked us. I'm captive.

"Arianna!" he called out. "Somebody!"

The room was solid concrete—the floor, the ceiling and the walls.

No one will hear me in here, no matter how loud I scream.

His breathing quickened and he started to panic. He touched the back of his head again.

Did they really implant a chip to steal my dreams?

He couldn't feel a cut or scar.

I don't know what's real and what's not anymore.

Then he heard something. A muffled noise, that he felt more than heard.

An explosion?

The room shook, bits of dust falling from the ceiling. He rushed back to the door. All he could see through the mesh in the door was a deserted corridor. Another explosion rocked the room but this time a wall of fire swept by the window and made him stumble back.

Solaris?

The sprinklers embedded in the roof sprang to life, cascading water that trickled into Sam's eyes, blinding him.

"Help! Somebody, help!" he screamed, certain that his voice would not be heard but there was little else he could do. As he stood there the door grew hot to the touch from the fire outside, the sprinklers out there seeming to do little against the raging inferno.

Sam banged helplessly against the locked door. "Get me out of here!"